Just One Chance

The Kingston Family
Book 3

NEW YORK TIMES BESTSELLING AUTHOR

Carly Phillips

JUST ONE CHANCE

He thought she was the one...until she walked away. Now she's back and he wants her more than ever.

As a former Marine, Xander Kingston's writing keeps him sane. Bonus? His thrillers made him one of Hollywood's most desired screenwriters—and also introduced him to a fledgling starlet who broke his heart. With his close-knit family in New York, Xander returned home and found peace. Until Sasha Keaton shows up at his Hamptons retreat. Now an A-Lister, she's as beautiful as he remembers. And just as dangerous to his heart.

Sasha learned from watching her mother to never sacrifice her dreams for anyone—only to discover how empty life could be without the man she loved. Now cast in Xander's latest movie, she needs his insight to play the part, but secretly hopes for a second chance.

Xander has built emotional walls to keep Sasha at a distance, but their physical attraction can't be denied. When a stalker's threats intensify, Xander moves Sasha into his house to keep her safe. Before long she's back in his bed and making inroads in his life.

But when the danger passes and the movie wraps, Sasha and Xander face a familiar choice—put career first or give love a fighting chance.

Chapter One

XANDER KINGSTON WOKE to the sound of voices in his backyard. His gated, locked pool area and the retreat he valued for its privacy. What day was it again? He'd been up late writing. Tuesday, he remembered. And no good reason for him to be awake yet.

With a groan, he tossed the covers and walked to the sliding glass doors off the family room, pulling on a pair of boxer briefs on the way—but not bothering with pants or shorts. If the overgrown idiots in his pool were going to interrupt his solitude, they could suck up the view.

His golden retriever, Bella, rose at the same time he did, and Xander paused to pet her on the head. "Hang on, girl. Let me just take care of something and we'll go for a run."

He opened the door and stepped onto the pool deck, letting Bella rush past the pool to the grass where she did her business.

"Hey! Go home to your place," Xander shouted at his company.

As he'd expected, his brother Dash and the other members of the Original Kings, an award-winning rock band, loved and beloved around the world, were hanging outside. For Xander, who'd been up late working on his latest thriller, he couldn't claim the same adoration. Especially since Dash had an equally huge house with a pool and the same amount of privacy a mile down the road.

"We needed a change of scenery to help unlock the muse," Jagger, the lead guitarist, called from his lounger in the pool.

"Sorry, man. Didn't mean to wake you," Dash said. "I just had an idea and had to sing it out to the boys. Listen." He picked up his guitar and played a riff while belting out an accompanying chorus.

Xander had to admit it was catchy. It also could have happened at Dash's house.

"I like it. I'm feeling the beat," Mac, the bass player, said, his hands moving in the air as if he were strumming his instrument.

"Where's Dominic?" Xander asked of their drummer.

The guys shot each other a look but no one answered.

Xander shook his head. The band wasn't his problem. At least today's visit didn't involve groupies and alcohol. "I hope you brought your own towels," he muttered, stepping back inside.

He quickly pulled on running shorts, a tank, and socks then laced up his sneakers. After washing up and taking care of things in the bathroom, he headed to the kitchen to find his brother pouring a glass of orange juice, Xander's morning favorite. He'd already made himself a cup of iced tea.

"Where are the guys?" Xander asked before picking up his drink and swallowing it quickly because he was thirsty. Bella obviously felt the same way, because she lapped at her water, the sound loud in the kitchen.

Dash gestured with his thumb. "They went back to my place." He took a sip of his drink. "So what crawled up your ass this morning?"

"I was up late." He leaned against the counter and glanced at his brother. "I didn't set an alarm and I didn't expect be woken up by you and the band."

"Didn't like being serenaded, huh?" Dash laughed. "Sorry. But you of all people know sometimes a change of scenery helps the creative process."

"And sometimes you show up because you'd just rather I be the one left with the clean-up." His brother was incorrigible. Xander supposed it came from their mother allowing Dash to cultivate his artistic talent instead of adhering to structure and rules.

Dash didn't deny it. "Hey, we still on for the family barbeque?"

"Yeah. Here on Saturday night." Normally their get-togethers were on Sundays, but since Xander's movie began filming in the city on Monday, he'd switched up the day.

Xander's family were a tight group, cared about what was going on in everyone else's lives, and made it a point to get together often. Linc, the oldest, liked to think he'd taken over the paternal role since their cheating father had been emotionally absent, but the three Kingston brothers, their sister, Chloe, and newly found half sister, Aurora, looked out for each other. Always.

Xander pushed himself off the counter. "I'm going for a run. You sticking around?"

Dash shook his head. "Nah. I think I'll head back to the guys. See what we can make work in the studio."

Before Xander could reply, his cell rang and he grabbed it from his pocket. His agent's name flashed on the screen. "Raye," he mouthed to his brother.

Raye Douglas, partner at Douglas Talent Management Group, had represented Xander ever since Dash had convinced *his* manager there to ask the best literary agent to read Xander's manuscript five years ago. Raye, the daughter of the top agent at the firm, had been curious, poached the script from her dad, and she'd been impressed.

Xander had been equally taken by her unwilling-ness to settle or take no for an answer. She'd pushed hard for him, and Xander had ended up in a bidding war that culminated in both publishing and movie rights being sold, making him a proverbial overnight success. After a grueling four years in the Marines, that is.

He accepted the call. "Hey, Raye."

"Good news. We have an actress to play Amanda," she said of Xander's protagonist's love interest.

His military thrillers were focused on a fictional character, Gavin Steele, a Marine in a special unit. In a prior book, Xander had killed off Steele's wife, and in the current novel and script, the new character of Amanda would be first an adversary, then Steele's love interest in what Xander planned to be an increasingly larger part.

The original actress slated to play Amanda had backed out at the last minute, and with filming set to start next week, the studio had been scrambling. They didn't want to settle but knew it would be tough to obtain a big name. Besides, Xander would be around to help her get into character.

"Who'd we get?" He glanced at Dash, who raised an eyebrow, clearly interested as well.

"Sasha Keaton," his agent said.

And with those words, Xander's brain short-circuited, and as he processed the news, his heart beat harder in his chest.

"Fuck no." He didn't have final say in casting, but he was allowed reasonable input, and he did not want the woman who'd put her career over their relationship and broken his heart working on his movie.

"Who'd they pick?" Dash asked. He knew Xander had been waiting on this news.

Xander held up a finger, buying himself time with his brother before replying.

"Excuse me," Raye said. "But are you telling me you're going to let the past dictate whether or not you accept the hottest actress in the country … screw that … in the world playing this role?" His agent asked a rational question.

Xander didn't have an equally rational answer. Ending things with Sasha had shattered his world as much as the IED that exploded too close to him in Afghanistan had blown up his military career.

"I need you to think," Raye said in the face of Xander's silence. "Sasha is a huge get and her signing will boost your desirability. Don't forget we're negotiating an option on your new series to a streaming service. You want the biggest names possible bringing in the largest numbers possible on your current project. And her face sells. Tickets, subscriptions, all of it."

Xander muttered under his breath. He didn't like it but Raye was right. Before he could acknowledge that fact, she spoke again. "Don't let your bruised ego stand in the way."

This movie was due to shoot in Manhattan, and as a consultant, Xander planned to be on set often. "Fuck." He ran a hand over his cropped hair and groaned. And despite his past with Sasha, he could be professional. "Fine," he muttered.

Raye let out a relieved, loud breath. "Catch up at lunch soon?" she asked.

"Yeah."

"Okay, take it easy. Remember, this is a good thing," she said before disconnecting without a goodbye. Typical Raye.

Xander set his phone on the counter, closed his eyes, and mentally counted to ten and back, the method he used to calm down when stressed. When he opened his eyes, Dash was staring at him with concern.

"You okay?"

Xander shrugged. "Pissed."

"I got that. Just as I figured from your reaction they want to hire Sasha for the role?"

He ran a hand over the back of his neck and nodded. "Raye reminded me it will only benefit me and the deals we're negotiating to have Sasha on board."

His gut churned at the thought of seeing her again. "But I'm not planning on dealing with her on set." He could be cordial and professional but that was it. He wasn't required to be friends with the actors. He'd just be there to make sure they stayed true to the characters he'd created.

Dash eyed him warily. "Well, I agree with your instinct to steer clear. She was career driven when you met her, and nothing we've seen in the last couple of years shows she's changed."

Xander nodded. It wasn't like he could miss learning about Sasha's life. Not the way she was constantly splashed across tabloids, social media, and the news. He'd wondered if she'd grown up, changed, and found other priorities, but Dash was right.

Every photo showed her hanging out with her male co-stars, every article and caption insinuating she had a tendency to relationship hop, and eventually Xander stopped paying attention.

Dash placed a hand on Xander's shoulder before dropping it. "I just wouldn't want her to hurt you again."

"She'd have to get close to me for that to happen." But he appreciated Dash's concern. "I need that run." He slid his phone into the armband he kept on his counter and velcroed it to his bicep. His Bose earbuds came next.

"You'll feel better after you pound out that frustration on the pavement." Dash slapped him on the back. "Hey, if you want to make Sasha jealous, I could introduce you to someone you can bring with you on set."

"A groupie?" Xander frowned, the idea holding no appeal. His brother's rock-star lifestyle was not for him, and someday it was going to catch up to his brother. "Thanks but no thanks," he said, though Dash had raised an eyebrow as if he'd really expected Xander to say yes.

Dash shrugged. "Your choice. Okay, I'm out of here, too. Yell if you need me."

"Will do," Xander said and walked out with his brother, Bella trotting alongside them.

SASHA KEATON FOLDED her favorite sleep shirt and placed it in her suitcase, followed by item after item on her bed. Beside her, Cassidy Forrester, her best friend and personal assistant, sat on the chair by Sasha's vanity area, her iPad open as they discussed travel arrangements for their trip to New York.

Sasha zipped her piece of luggage closed, ignoring the twisting in her stomach every time she thought about the man whose movie she'd accepted a part in.

"So, we leave tomorrow at nine twenty a.m. and

land around six New York time," Cassidy said, reading off the itinerary. "We're staying at the Gansevoort, with you in a one-bedroom suite with an outdoor terrace, and I have an adjoining king room next door."

"Excellent. You'll have your own space to sleep, and we can hang out in the suite."

Sasha met Cassidy when she'd answered an ad for a room in a two-bedroom apartment after she'd wrapped a movie in France. She'd returned to LA coming off a breakup she didn't want to think about now but would have to deal with soon. In Cassidy, Sasha had found both a roommate and a best friend at a low point in her life.

Then, as Sasha's career exploded, Cassidy had been by her side, using her skills to run Sasha's personal life and business schedule, something she'd done for her brother, Axel, a drummer, who also lived in LA. But despite Cassidy and Sasha's professional relationship, their friendship came first, and Sasha felt like she'd known Cassidy forever.

Cassidy left the iPad on the table and joined Sasha, curling a leg beneath her on the bed. "When are we going to talk about it?"

"About what?" Sasha played dumb, but her friend wouldn't accept her silence about Xander for much longer.

"When I met you, you were pretty broken up

about the guy. Now you're starring in a movie based on a book he wrote and he'll be a consultant on set? You haven't said one word about him since taking the part. I thought I'd wait until you were ready, but we're leaving in the morning so … time's up." Cassidy treated Sasha to a pointed stare.

Sasha settled on the mattress near her friend, pushing aside the suitcase and resigning herself to the conversation she'd been avoiding. When she'd moved in with Cassidy, she'd been an emotional mess, and she'd had only herself to blame. She bit down on her cheek at the painful memory. At the time, she'd cried and gorged on ice cream, and Cassidy, even as a new friend, had been there, supporting her.

Sasha had explained everything about her relationship and breakup, and Cassidy had understood. She hadn't judged her then and she wouldn't now. Since Sasha intended to see Xander before she walked onto the set, she'd need a plan and some good, solid advice.

She drew a deep breath and slid her hand over the ruffles on her comforter. "You know that when I met Xander, I wasn't in the right headspace for a relationship. I had goals I wanted to achieve. And I definitely didn't see anyone like him coming into my life."

She recalled being at a party at Raye Douglas' home. Sasha had been invited by someone so low on the totem pole she'd been certain she'd be asked to leave or not allowed in. The house had been huge, a decorator's dream, beyond anything Sasha had ever seen in her life, and the guests were household names.

She'd felt so out of place, and when the handsome guy with a military bearing strode up to her and began to make conversation, she'd been relieved to no longer be alone. The sparks flew from the moment they'd locked eyes as he'd approached. They ended up in a small corner area, sitting and talking for most of the night. Sasha had grabbed champagne glass after champagne glass off the passing caterers' trays as they got to know each other.

To her shock, they'd fallen into a relationship, but Sasha had dreams, the main one not to give up herself and her career the way her mother had, to follow her musician father around wherever a gig took him.

And then came Xander.

Knowing she'd gotten lost in the past, she glanced at Cassidy. "I need to see him before shooting starts. To clear the air if nothing else. I can't show up the first day I have to be in character and have the pressure of dealing with him hanging over me."

Even if the thought of meeting him face-to-face for the first time since they'd broken up turned her stomach. "Besides, if there's an author for the story and they're an on-set consultant, you know I like to get their take on the character I'm playing. It makes it easier to get into their skin.''

Cassidy's expression grew serious. "Are you over him? Because this can get messy. I worried when you took the role and—"

"I love Isaac Reynolds," she said of the director. "The last time I worked with him was a dream. They lost their leading actress, and the movie is a guaranteed blockbuster. Every Steele movie is."

But Cassidy pursed her lips, studying Sasha intently. "You didn't mention Xander in your reasons, and I don't believe for a minute that seeing him again didn't factor into your decision."

Sasha clenched her hands. "So what if it did?" She'd never forgotten him and had always wanted the chance to make things right.

"There'll be more Steele movies. This character is a long-term commitment," Cassidy reminded her.

Sasha's stomach clenched. "I'm aware."

"So you wanted to see him again. And again and again?"

Sasha picked up a pillow and tossed it at her friend. "Stop. I just need to know he doesn't hate me." And maybe she still wanted him to have feelings for her, too.

She didn't know and wouldn't until she saw him face-to-face. Not that it mattered. He wouldn't want anything to do with her beyond the movie. She'd hurt him badly in so many ways.

The truth was, she'd been all of nineteen, new to Hollywood, wanting to make it big, and had both her agent and her co-star pushing her to do things that would keep the media focus on them. Make them look important. Help them become hot commodities.

It'd been so hard to say no to their ideas and plans. They'd kept her so busy she didn't have time to overthink her choices or even see Xander often enough to make a relationship work. And she'd also had her mother's voice in her head, telling her not to make the mistakes she had. Reminding her to follow her dreams, that love was fleeting. And then she'd point out all Sasha's father's misdeeds.

And her life wasn't much different now. Her days were hectic, busy, and she was constantly on the go.

"Hey. What's going on?" Cassidy asked, interrupting Sasha's thoughts. "Is it just that Xander stirred up old memories that's got you thrown?"

Sasha rose to her feet and paced her bedroom. "No. I mean that's some of it, but I just wrapped up one movie and I expected to have some time off, then this role came up and I jumped at the opportunity." The chance to see Xander, to work near him, had been impossible to resist. "But if it had been anything else?" She glanced up and shook her head. "I'm tired, Cass."

Going from one film to the next, moving countries, cities, rarely being here in the home she'd bought and decorated. Her mother lived in a guesthouse on the property, which let Sasha see her when she was around, but it wasn't often.

Cassidy was in tune with her feelings and obviously sensed Sasha needed to talk, so she remained silent and listened. When the time came for her opinion, Cass never had trouble giving it, even if it was something Sasha wouldn't want to hear.

"It's like I'm living a life most people would envy, yet as much as I hate to admit it, I feel … empty. And that makes me feel guilty and ungrateful because look how much I have." She gestured around to her big bedroom with the most comfortable bed she could own and the décor of her dreams in cream and white with touches of pale pink. She wasn't living her dreams, she'd exceeded them.

Cassidy rose and stepped over to her. "You set up a charity for kids in the downtown areas. You provide computers to schools and clothes for people who can't afford it when their children outgrow what they own. You're doing good with what you have. Stop it with the guilt. But I am concerned about everything you're saying. If you're not happy…"

Sasha shrugged and pulled in a deep breath of air. "I'm excited about this role. Whatever happens next, let's just say we'll see. Maybe I'll slow down, take a break, reevaluate."

"Your agent is not going to take you slowing down well. Neither will your mother."

Cassidy was correct. Sasha's mom had already lit into her for accepting a role that brought Xander back into her life, warning her not to get involved with him again, not to let a man derail her career and all she'd worked for. And Rebecca Burton, her agent, was all about keeping up momentum while Sasha was hot.

Sasha groaned, not wanting to deal with their pressure, either. "I'll worry about them later. How about you? Would you have a problem if I didn't jump into another movie right away?"

"Hell no. I'm team Sasha all the way." Cassidy gave her a bright smile. "Now let's talk about you seeing Xander. What's your plan?"

Sasha laid out her agenda. "Filming starts next week."

She only had two weeks on set because this movie was her character's introduction to the franchise. She'd have more screen time with each consecutive movie. At least, that was how the role had been pitched to her.

She glanced at Cassidy, who was waiting for her to continue. "We're getting in early, like I always do before shooting, to get a feel for the city we're in, the people we're working with on set. And in this case, with so little time, I'd like the man who created the character to give me insight into how she thinks and who she is."

A smile lifted Cassidy's lips. "Xander."

Sasha nodded. "Xander. But I have to break the ice first. We have to talk and get to a point where we can work together. So I'm going to have to surprise him and hope he doesn't throw me out." Nerves assaulted her at the mere thought of approaching him again for the first time in years.

"Do you have his address?"

"As a matter of fact, I do." She and Xander didn't share an agent because they weren't in the same line of work. But they shared a talent agency, and it hadn't been difficult to pull some strings and find out where Xander lived and in which of his residences he was currently staying.

Now she just needed to gather her courage and show up on his doorstep.

Chapter Two

S ASHA'S PLANE LANDED at 6:10 p.m. at JFK International Airport, and from there, she and Cassidy waited for their luggage. In a pair of jeans and a man-style shirt with a baseball cap on her head and sunglasses over her eyes, Sasha did her best not to meet anyone's gaze and hoped she could remain anonymous.

She'd flown under her legal name, Alexandra Keaton. Sasha had been her Russian mother's nickname for her, and she'd taken it as her stage name. Using an Uber with Cassidy's account and staying under an alias at the hotel protected her even more.

She hated the idea of having a bodyguard around twenty-four seven nor did she think it necessary. Plenty of A-list celebrities flew without an entourage, and that was the way Sasha wanted to live. It was enough she boarded via a special terminal that had a separate door from which to enter the plane. Some perks were worth it and necessary.

Beside her, Cassidy dressed similarly, and with her blond hair, she and Sasha looked like sisters. They grabbed their bags and took an Uber to the hotel in the Meatpacking District in New York City, remaining under the radar almost the entire time.

As they walked outside to their Uber, hot, humid, New York air surrounded her. Although it was late June, the weather had that mid-summer, sticky feel.

They stepped toward the sidewalk and Sasha felt the weight of someone's stare. She turned to see a brown haired man in a baseball cap a few feet from her. She thought he'd ducked his head and focused on his phone as she glanced over but couldn't be certain he'd ever seen her. Paranoia at its finest, she mused, still not used to the stares even after a couple of years.

Once settled in the suite, Sasha relaxed, tossing her hat onto the couch in the main lounge area.

"Long flights are a bitch," Cassidy muttered, doing the same.

"Amen." Sasha flopped onto the sofa beside their caps, kicked off her Chucks, and groaned. "Let's order in dinner."

After they decided on their meals and Cassidy placed an order, they talked until the food arrived. It wasn't until Sasha was alone in her room, washing up, that she allowed herself to face her plans for tomorrow.

Seeing Xander wouldn't be easy but it was necessary. Both for her professional sense of comfort when portraying his character and for her to make things right.

XANDER WOKE UP to blessed silence. The band had obviously stayed at Dash's house this morning. After his normal a.m. routine, he and Bella made their daily run into town, circled around, and headed back home.

Nearing the end, Xander slowed to a walk and whistled to Bella, who'd gotten ahead of him, to do the same. The humidity was high and sweat poured down his body. Lifting his shirt, he wiped his face and looked forward to stepping inside and feeling the air conditioner cooling him off.

As he approached his house, he saw a car in the driveway and someone sitting on his front porch. His eyes weren't what they used to be, not since the severe concussion he'd received from being too close to an IED blast in Afghanistan. His glasses, which he only wore when his eyes hurt from exhaustion, usually after too much writing, were inside.

He didn't recognize the car but kept to a walk, not wanting to push Bella too hard in this heat. As he drew closer, whoever sat on the wicker chair rose, and he realized a woman stood waiting for him. A slender woman with blond hair pulled back in a ponytail, sunglasses covering her eyes, and a sleeveless dress that hugged familiar curves walked down the three steps to the path leading to the driveway.

Sasha.

Fuck.

She looked beautiful. The black dress was cute and fitted, with sunflowers on the skirt and a small one on the tight top, ending just above the knee. With her hair back, she appeared young and as vulnerable as she had the night they'd met. His heart, already beating hard from his run, picked up speed, and he damned the effect she had on him.

He had no intention of rushing and giving her the wrong impression, but his dog hadn't gotten the memo and she took off at a run. Traitor.

Bella had failed at becoming an emotional service dog because she hadn't been able to ignore distractions, as proven by her run and now jump on Sasha. Since Xander's issues weren't serious in comparison to many who'd enlisted and come home, Xander had chosen Bella and her quirks, leaving the trained dogs to those who might need them more.

"Bella, down!"

At the sound of his voice and command, his girl placed all four paws on the ground and sat, but she quivered with the need to jump on their guest again.

"Sorry," Xander said to Sasha. "She's a little exuberant, even with strangers."

She treated him to a soft smile. "It's okay. She's sweet." She reached out and petted his dog's head. "What's her name?"

"Bella."

"Meaning *beautiful* in any language," Sasha murmured, obviously aware that the name was Latin and related in some way to that word in all the Romance languages.

She *was* beautiful. Not just his dog but Sasha herself. The woman who didn't care if a dog with dusty paws, dirty from a run, jumped on her designer dress. Because she could now afford to upgrade her clothes, and this outfit looked high quality, unlike the Target outfits she'd attempted to dress up once upon a time.

And he didn't want to notice anything about her. Not the good similarities to the past or the changes in the present. "What are you doing here?" he asked in a gruffer voice than he'd used before.

She folded her arms across her chest, running her palms over her bare skin on her forearms. "I thought we should talk." She lifted one delicate shoulder as if that explained everything. "You know, because we'll be working together."

Not if he could help it. He intended to stay far away. "A little warning before showing up would have been nice."

To her credit, she didn't flinch. But then she was

an actress. It was easy to pretend.

"Why? So you could make sure you weren't home? Or make certain you didn't come back?" Her gaze traveled over him, her eyes darkening at the sight of him in his running shorts, tank, and sneakers.

She clearly liked what she saw. So did he, but sexual attraction meant nothing in the wake of hurt and fundamental differences.

At the reminder, he let out a groan. The sooner they *talked*, the sooner she'd get in her rental car and leave. Buying time, he glanced over to the lush green lawn where Bella was sniffing the grass. He had no doubt he was going to wind up with another brown spot, because another thing about Bella, she squatted where it suited her.

Women, he thought to himself, frustrated. They always got their way.

"What did you want to discuss?" he asked coldly. Because he couldn't imagine he and Sasha had much to say to each other.

She met his gaze and lifted her glasses, revealing those stunning blue eyes he'd always been able to get lost in.

"I can't get into character if I'm on edge because you're being an ass and glaring at me." The first glimmer of insecurity flashed in her eyes. "I thought we could…"

"I'm not rehashing the past," he said, cutting her off.

She swallowed hard. "Fine. Then can we call a truce? Look," she said, reaching out as if to touch him and immediately snatching her hand back. "I need your input on Amanda's character. It's something I like to do when I'm in a movie based on a novel and the author is going to be on set. It's important I meet everyone's expectations. Including yours."

Goddammit. Xander might be able to put up a wall between them personally, but he *was* being a dick professionally and that wasn't acceptable. If she couldn't play the part because of him, the movie based on his novel would suffer. She probably knew she had him on that point but was smart enough not to show it with a smirk or knowing look.

"So can I come in?" she asked, gesturing to the front of his house.

His Hamptons retreat that, unlike his Manhattan apartment, city crowds, and noise, didn't trigger his lingering anxiety from combat. He wouldn't call it PTSD exactly. He just needed peace, quiet, and solitude. And Sasha, the woman who'd broken his heart, now wanted to invade his sanctuary, ensuring she'd leave her presence and scent behind.

WELL, THAT WENT worse than she'd thought it would. Sasha followed Xander and his obedient, sweet dog up the couple of stairs to the porch, waiting while he unlocked his door and let them inside.

He tossed the keys into a bowl on a credenza and turned. "I'm going to take a quick shower. I'll be right back."

Nodding, she glanced around as he walked into the house and toward what she presumed was the master bedroom. The interior was furnished with what she'd call man-style Hamptons' flair. An open-concept first floor took her from the entry area to the massive living/family room with windows overlooking the beach.

Bella stepped across the floor, her nails tapping as she moved, and she disappeared into what Sasha assumed was the kitchen. The loud sound of lapping water followed and she knew she was right. Bella was drinking in the other room.

Continuing to appraise Xander's house, Sasha took in the smooth dark-stained wood floors that ran through every room. A white sofa and chairs made the open area feel cozy, the warm atmosphere helped by white antique-styled leather trunk end and coffee tables with brass buckles, locks, and hinges.

She doubted Xander had decorated himself and assumed his sister, Chloe, or his mother had given him a hand. Sasha much preferred that thought to considering another woman helping him make this place a home.

Bella's clicking nails announced her arrival. Xander hadn't had a dog when he was in LA, and Sasha wondered how long after coming back he'd gotten the pup. A cold nose nudged her bare legs, and Bella leaned her warm body against Sasha's legs. Bending down, Sasha petted the soft fur before turning her attention to the framed family photos set around the room.

With so many siblings, Xander had plenty of pictures. To keep busy and not overthink the cool welcome he'd given her, she glanced at the photos, recognizing Xander's mother, brothers, and sister she'd met when they'd traveled to LA to visit him. As an only child, Sasha had been overwhelmed by his big family and envied him at the same time.

Her gaze fell to an unfamiliar younger woman in one of the frames. Long blond hair fell to the bottom of her back, big blue eyes stared at the camera, and a wide smile was on her pretty face. In another picture, the same woman held an infant in her arms, Xander by her side with an arm around her waist.

Sasha picked up the photo, studying it, shocked and confused because she didn't recognize the woman as anyone in his family. She had the momentary thought that Xander might have a wife and a baby, a possibility she'd never allowed herself to consider. Xander moving on hadn't crossed her mind and it should have.

A pang twisted inside her, and she braced one palm against her abdomen.

"You okay?" Xander's voice sounded as he walked into the room, and Bella's tail began to wag as she greeted him, rubbing her body against his legs the same way she'd done to Sasha.

He glanced at the photo in her hand. "What are you doing?"

She ran her tongue over her dry lips. "I ... ummm ... I was just looking around." She tipped her head to the side. "Is that, I mean, is the baby yours?"

He stared at her in shock. "No," he said at last. "Aurora is my half sister. We found out about her this past year. The baby is hers."

Oh, God. A sister. She felt so stupid. And relieved.

He plucked the frame out of her hand and set it back on the shelf.

She finally let herself look at him and wished she hadn't. He'd been sexy as hell in his running gear, but now, shirtless in a pair of track pants, his body muscled and tanned, his hair damp from the shower, heat slammed into her hard.

Along with desire, memories of their time together

came flooding back. The good times, not the bad ones at the end. Waking up late to see him working on his laptop, the sun streaming in from the apartment window. His big hand gripping her neck, those delicious lips on hers, and his naked body covering her, blanketing her in heat.

"Can I get you something to drink?" His gruff voice interrupted her thoughts.

She shook her head. "No, thanks."

"Then what can I do for you, Sasha? Seriously. What do you want?"

So many things but none that made any sense, she thought. "I would love it if you could give me insight into Amanda. I read the book—"

"You did?" Surprise etched his features.

She nodded. "I read what you wrote while we were together, so yeah. I continued to read your books ... after."

After she'd lost the man she loved because she'd been unable to handle him and her career. She'd pretty much proved she couldn't have it all. Not a career on an upward trajectory, a man who hated the spotlight and who preferred a solitary, quiet life, and professionals around her, not to mention her own mother, pushing her in a direction that hadn't included Xander.

She forced herself to clear those thoughts, aware her cheeks were hot as she admitted she'd kept him in her life in her own way.

"Anyway, I read the book but it's in Steele's point of view, which means I don't really get to know the new woman in his life. I know how she acts, that she's strong, can handle a man who's often in danger, but I don't have a handle on how she *feels*."

"I can understand that," he said, the words reluctantly drawn from him. "So how can I help?"

She drew a deep breath. "Filming starts next week. Can we spend some time together talking about the character?" She glanced up at him, feeling the tug of desire as she looked into his deep blue eyes. The beard covering his face was new but lent an air of increased sexiness to a man who already oozed plenty of raw masculinity.

They still stood by the shelf with the photos. He appeared tired from his run, and she could see the internal war he fought with himself as he thought about her request.

"Purely for the movie's sake," she assured him. "Maybe you could come into the city one night for an early dinner? We can walk around the area where we'll be filming. Where Steele lives. It'll help me get in character while we talk." She wasn't lying, either.

True, she'd love to spend time with him, just because. For no reason other than wanting to get him to open up to her again, see how he was doing. How his headaches were, if he still needed his glasses. But he didn't want to give her that kind of privilege and she accepted it. She did, however, need his author's insight.

"Sure," he said at last. "I'll come in Friday night. Does that work for you?"

Today was Thursday. She and Cassidy wanted to do some shopping, and she needed time alone to study her lines. The timing gave her all day tomorrow.

"Sure, that works great." She pulled her phone out of the small purse hanging from her shoulder. "Umm, I got a new phone number. Not that I think you still have my old one or anything. I just had a problem with some rabid fan hacking my information."

His gaze narrowed into angry slits. "Are you here with a bodyguard?" he asked.

She shook her head. "I only take them to major events. I'm with my assistant, Cassidy. She's my best friend. And we play it smart. I'm fine."

Still scowling, he took her cell and put his number into it then hit send. His phone rang in the bedroom, giving him her number, too. Neither one of them discussed further whether or not they'd deleted each other's numbers *after*. She was coming to hate that word.

He handed her phone back.

"Thank you." She tucked the cell into her bag.

Since he wasn't making conversation, she took that as her cue. "I should get going. It's a long drive back to the city."

He nodded and walked her to the door, the scent of his soap and hint of warm scented aftershave causing desire to do a slow glide through her veins.

He opened the front door for her, and at the sound, Bella came skidding across the floor and nudged her nose into Sasha's leg as if to say, *Were you really going to leave without saying goodbye?*

Unable to help herself, Sasha dropped to her knees, cupped the dog's muzzle in her hand, and kissed her nose. "Take care, sweet girl."

She rose to her feet and met Xander's warm gaze. "Thank you," she said with as much sincerity as she could muster. She wanted him to know how much she appreciated his time. Time he was begrudgingly giving. "I really appreciate you helping me."

He let out a small grunt she couldn't quite interpret. "Where are you staying?" he asked.

"The Gansevoort. Text me once you're in the lobby." She bit down on the inside of her cheek.

"I will." He braced a hand on the door, his sexy body too hot for her to keep staring at. "I'll be by around five tomorrow."

Despite his lack of enthusiasm, her stomach flipped with anticipation. She tempered the emotion, reminding herself he was doing her a favor so the movie would be successful. Nothing more.

He'd given her no opening today, no *in*, *nothing*. No matter how much she wished otherwise.

SASHA RETURNED TO the hotel, where Cassidy was making some calls and arranging things to be available in Sasha's trailer on set. She wasn't a diva and didn't put a ton of demands into her contract, but there were some reasonable items she requested. Despite her mother's push to do otherwise, she'd wanted to be known as someone who was easy to work with and be offered more roles as a result.

"Hey," Sasha said, letting the suite door slam shut behind her.

"Oh my God, you're back!" Cassidy placed her laptop onto the table and jumped up from her seat on the sofa. "Tell me everything. How did he look? Was he surprised to see you? Was he welcoming?"

Sasha strode over and sunk into a comfortable chair. "Amazing, yes, and sort of? He didn't send me home without listening to what I had to say. But welcoming? Not so much."

"Oh, damn. Can I get you a drink?" Cassidy asked.

"Actually, I'd prefer to grab something to eat. I'm starving." Her stomach had been grumbling the entire trip back. She refused to think the uncomfortable sensation had anything to do with Xander's aloof attitude.

Cassidy nodded. "Order room service or go downstairs?"

"Downstairs. I don't want to be cooped up here forever. After our late lunch, I need to run lines." Where all she would do was think about Xander and analyze everything he'd said.

"Let me ensure we get a private table where no one will bother you. Be right back." Cassidy headed over to the room phone and made the call.

Sasha tipped her head against the back of the chair. God, she was lucky to have Cassidy in her life. The best friend a girl could want and an amazing assistant who didn't have an ounce of jealousy inside her. She was truly happy for Sasha's seemingly overnight success.

When Sasha had moved into the small apartment with Cassidy, her new roommate had been working for an ad agency, and after Sasha's sudden rise, Cassidy had been thrilled to become her personal assistant. And when Sasha bought a house in LA, she'd had Cassidy move in. There were plenty of rooms and enough privacy to go around.

"All set! Let's go eat."

A little while later, they were sitting inside at the

Chester on the ground floor of the hotel. Cassidy had known to ask for indoor seating, skipping the outside biergarten that wrapped around the exterior. Sasha wanted privacy and she hoped she'd skip any autograph requests, but if someone asked, she rarely said no. The fans bought tickets to see her in her movies, after all.

She'd finished her grilled chicken sandwich with a tasty aioli sauce and an iced tea. Not wanting to discuss Xander, Sasha turned the subject to Cassidy's boyfriend.

"Is Adam still giving you a hard time about being in New York?" Cassidy and Adam had been together since before Sasha had moved in. He'd been used to her having nine-to-five hours, and that wasn't the case anymore.

Cassidy, who was stirring her soda, looked up and sighed. "He doesn't understand the job. Or he doesn't want to understand. I get that he feels neglected. I just don't know what to tell him."

Sasha leaned forward in her seat. "Do you want to go back? You can work from there, and I can always hire someone for when I travel." She'd hate it but she would make it work for her friend.

"No." Cassidy spoke immediately. "I love what I do and I love working with you. And traveling. This isn't something I'd get to do otherwise, see foreign countries and stay at an upscale hotel. I was hoping he'd understand and wait. It's not like we're a married couple with a family. This is the time for me to do this."

Sasha relaxed. "Okay. I just don't want to be responsible for messing up your relationship."

"And you aren't."

That settled, they gestured for a check and signed the bill with a generous tip to Sasha's room.

As she stood up, Sasha felt an eerie prickle wash over her and glanced around.

Cassidy, who had started walking out, turned and headed back to where Sasha still stood. "What's wrong?"

She shivered and shook her head, feeling silly. "I just had this weird feeling like someone was watching me. Which is insane because people notice me all the time." They snapped photos on their phone without her permission. But this felt different.

Cassidy turned, her gaze scanning the room. "I don't see anyone looking or anything odd, but come on. Let's get you out of here." They started for the door when Cassidy asked, "Are you sure you don't want a bodyguard?"

She shook her head. "I'm being ridiculous. The set has security and nobody knows I'm in town."

So far there'd been no paparazzi or anyone outright noticing her. She wasn't dressed up and hadn't looked anyone in the eye. Just acting like a regular person in the city. It wouldn't last. It never did, but for now she was fine, and whatever odd sensation she'd felt a few seconds ago was gone.

They went back to their rooms to wash up and get into comfortable clothes, and for the next couple of hours, they hung out in the suite and Sasha and Cassidy ran lines.

She wasn't completely comfortable with the character, and she knew why. Because a script never completely conveyed the depth and thoughts of the person, and she needed more insight. More than even reading the book had given her. When a movie was an adaptation, she hesitated to put her own spin on it completely. Even Isaac, the director, had told her to meet with the author because he had contractual input. Which meant she needed an in-depth take on Amanda's personality.

She needed Xander.

Chapter Three

S ASHA AND CASSIDY had spent the day shopping, starting early. Although Sasha had purchased a couple of outfits she might want to wear tonight, as she stared at the huge pile of clothes on her bed, she was no closer to deciding what to wear to go out to dinner with Xander.

She was being ridiculous since he wouldn't notice her clothing. She'd be lucky if he noticed *how* she looked at all. If their time together was like yesterday, he'd sit with a clenched jaw and stare past her with an *I no longer give a damn* look on his face.

Frowning, she decided on a navy and white polka-dotted skirt. A ruffle hit mid-thigh, and a matching loose top fluttered at the bottom, creating a cropped look if she lifted her arms. She grabbed a reasonable-height neutral colored heel in case they walked because … the city … and a small purse.

"How many more times are you going to change outfits?" Cassidy asked, an amused smile on her face as she entered the room.

"This is it." Sasha gestured to her cute skirt outfit.

Picking up a tube of lipstick, she strode to the mirror, swiped a hot-pink color over her lips, and pressed them together.

"Well, you look great. I know I suggested a professional blow-dry and glam, but you don't need it. You've got the talent to handle things yourself." Cassidy's smile helped Sasha relax despite the butterflies in her stomach at the thought of spending time with Xander.

"I don't want him to think I'm *that* girl anymore," she said. The one who cared so much about appearances and making it in Hollywood that she made the wrong choices and hurt people in the process.

Cassidy leaned against the doorframe, her head tipped to one side as she studied Sasha. "I met that girl and now she's my best friend. Do you really think that would have happened if there was something wrong with how you behaved? Or dressed? Or…" She stepped all the way into the room. "I think you're too hard on yourself about how and why things ended between the two of you."

Sasha frowned. "Maybe. Maybe not. But the fact remains, I'm more centered now." She trusted her own judgment a lot more than she ever had and did her best not to let other people influence her decisions.

Her cell rang and she picked it up off the bed, staring at the word *Mom* on the screen. As if Annika Keaton knew her daughter had been thinking about her.

"Ignore it," Cassidy said, aware of how insistent Sasha's mother could be.

Not manipulative per se. Annika just thought she knew what was best for Sasha based on her own mistakes.

Sasha shook her head. "She'll just keep calling." She picked up her cell and accepted the call. "Hi, Mom."

"Hi, honey. How's New York?"

"Great. The hotel is so much fun. It's decorated so beautifully. High ceilings in the suite, bay windows, and Cassidy has an attached room. It's all good."

Her mother talked about how she'd filmed as an extra in Manhattan before changing the subject to the one Sasha had been dreading. "So have you talked to *him*?"

Sasha sighed. "Yes, Mother, I've spoken to Xander. We're meeting up soon to discuss the character I'll be playing, and before you ask anything else, further questions are off-limits."

There was no way she could focus and do her job if her mother kept calling to remind her to be careful, not to make the same errors she had.

"I'm just looking out for you," her mom said.

"I appreciate it, but I don't need you to worry. I'm an adult and I know what I'm doing. And now I need to go or I'm going to be late. I love you and I'll talk to you soon."

"But–"

"Bye, Mom." Sasha disconnected the call, tossed the cell onto the comforter, and met Cassidy's gaze. "Well, that was fun."

Her friend laughed. "You've learned to handle her well."

Her phone buzzed again from its facedown position on the bed. "If my mother is calling back to give her opinion…" Sasha flipped the phone over and saw Xander's name flash on the screen along with a text.

She wasn't sure whether to be relieved or to get worked up again, this time for a wholly different reason. "Looks like my– Looks like Xander's here."

Cassidy raised her eyebrows. "Tell me you weren't about to say *date*."

Ignoring her, Sasha lifted her phone from the bed and replied she'd come down to the lobby. She grabbed her handbag and met her friend's gaze. "I'm leaving."

Cassidy waved, wriggling her fingers. "Be good!"

Sasha rolled her eyes and strode past her friend, the butterflies in her stomach growing by the second.

"I'm kidding, you know that right?" Cassidy asked.

"If you need to talk about anything, I'm here."

She turned back toward the bedroom, where Cassidy stood in the doorway. "I do. I'm just a nervous mess. I'll see you later."

Making her way down to the lobby, Sasha caught sight of Xander standing by a pillar. He wore a pair of jeans that showed off his toned physique. A black tee shirt hugged the muscles in his upper arms and chest, and a pair of loafers were on his feet. His dark brown hair was cropped short, same as when they'd met.

He rarely spoke about his military service, but she was aware of the tension that often consumed him in crowds of people. His hair was just part of his routine and who he'd become while in the Marines.

A pair of sunglasses hung from the neck of his shirt, and as if he felt her staring, he raised his gaze to meet hers. Between his chiseled features, full lips, and piercing stare, he was so sexy, any self-respecting female with a pulse would notice him.

He pushed himself off the pillar and strode over to meet her. "Hey," he said at the same time she said, "Hi."

She smiled.

He didn't but his intense expression unnerved her.

She fidgeted, wondering how to break the ice, then decided to just ignore his mood and the walls he obviously intended to keep in place. "I thought we could take a walk and talk about Amanda? Her motivations, who she is, things like that?"

He inclined his head. "That works. I made an early reservation at Serafina," he said. "It's pizza and Italian food. And I asked for a private booth so we won't be mobbed by people." He paused. "Unless you'd prefer to be out in the open?"

He spoke as if his question was more of an already made assumption, and she waved a hand, dismissing the idea. He had good reason to wonder if she'd want to be in the spotlight. There'd been a time when her goal was to see and be seen. But not anymore.

"God no," she said. "So far I've been able to stay under the radar here, and I hope to keep it that way."

He raised an eyebrow. "You do realize this hotel is known as a celebrity hangout?"

She nodded. "But it came highly recommended, and it's in walking distance of the Highline, the Chelsea Market, the Whitney Museum, *and* the West Village. And the beds? Have you ever stayed here? I've never slept on a more comfortable mattress," she said, trailing off as she caught how his eyes had darkened when she started talking about *beds*.

Which, now that she thought about it, had *her* recalling *them* and all the things they used to do on his large king mattress in LA. She shivered at the memory of his warm skin against hers, the scent of the aftershave he still wore, and the way his body had always commanded hers. Every part of her reacted, and she was grateful the navy top prevented him from noticing her hardened nipples.

She placed a hand on her hip, refocusing on their conversation about the hotel. "Point being, I really wanted to stay here for various reasons. So did you leave Bella in the Hamptons?" she asked, grasping for an easy change of subject.

"No. She's at my apartment uptown."

"You have a place in the city, too?" she asked, feigning surprise. No need to explain she'd called in favors to find out where he lived and where to find him. She was sure he already assumed as much.

He nodded. "Linc lives here. Chloe lives here, though now she's way downtown with Beck. That's her fiancé. Business brings me into the city since my agent is here, being bi-coastal and all. And the Hamptons is too long a trip to make for a brief business meeting."

She laughed at that. "Yes. I made the round trip in one day. I can attest to that." By the time she'd returned to Manhattan in her rented car, her legs had been numb.

"Besides, it's too damned busy in the city," he muttered.

She'd known he didn't like loud noises and crowds.

A walk was a bad idea. "I'm sorry. Would you rather just go to the restaurant, sit down, and talk there?"

He hesitated before nodding in agreement. "How about we just walk directly to the restaurant, and we can talk over an early dinner?"

"Compromise. I like it." Not waiting for him to reply, she deliberately hooked her arm into his and took that first step.

They strode out of the hotel and onto Ninth Avenue. She engaged him in conversation, asking how his family was doing but saving the sensitive questions about his new sister for later. Whatever the story behind Aurora's sudden appearance, Sasha was certain it was touchy and personal. And maybe not something Xander would want to discuss with her right now.

They arrived at the restaurant, and although it was early, a small group of people gathered around the hostess stand. Xander waited his turn and she stood beside him.

Just as he stepped up to the counter, Sasha heard her name and the whispers around her. She briefly closed her eyes and kept her gaze forward, hoping whoever had noticed her would be content with the sighting.

"Excuse me," a female voice said, this time much closer. Sasha turned, and girls about her age suddenly surrounded her.

"It's her," one of them whispered to the other.

Sasha understood that these women and others like them, not to mention men, were her audience and had made her career. Assuming her *I'm on* personality, she smiled at them, making them feel important. "Hi!" she said.

"Oh my God. Nobody will believe this. Can we take pictures with you?" one of them asked.

"And can I get your autograph?" another one requested, her voice more of a squeal.

At that point, the girls had drawn a crowd, and for the next … Sasha wasn't certain how long, she took requisite selfies, posed when other people snapped photos for each other, signed napkins, checks, and anything else the crowd came up with.

Finally, a manager stepped in and asked everyone to take their seats and allow her to enjoy her meal in peace. As everyone walked away, she let out a long breath, dropping her shoulders in relief.

She hadn't experienced the odd sensation of someone watching her in that creepy way again, but this crush of people, though she was used to it, set her off inside, causing anxiety.

Then she looked up and saw Xander standing against a wall, arms folded over his chest, an unreadable look on his handsome face, and nerves twisted her stomach for an entirely different reason.

★   ★   ★

NO SOONER HAD Xander given his name for their reservation than he turned to find Sasha surrounded by people, pushing to get a piece of her. He watched her flash a winning smile at her fans as she signed and took pictures without complaining for a solid thirty minutes.

The sight reminded him of the frenzied type of life she lived and thrived on, the same kind of life and choices that had broken them up in the first place.

He stood back and waited, the way he would have waited for her had they stayed together. Except she'd never managed to show him she could love or prioritize him in the same way.

While he stood to the side, he couldn't help but study her. Their time together used to be spent mostly in bed. Sexually they were completely compatible, which was the main reason he tried not to focus on how delectable she looked now in her outfit with the strip of bare skin that occasionally appeared when she'd move or lift her arms to sign something for a fan.

But the longer he watched her, the more he realized something about her was different. Beneath the act she put on for the crowd, there was a strain around her eyes and a tightness to that luscious pink-tinted mouth. And if he allowed himself to admit he looked close enough, a sadness he hadn't expected.

Given how much she'd wanted this kind of fame, he was surprised, but it wasn't his place to put an end to the circus. It did, however, make him wonder why she didn't travel with security to prevent her from being overwhelmed.

Finally, a large man who Xander assumed was the manager strode over and announced it was time for everyone to let Sasha sit down and eat in peace. He sure as hell had taken his sweet time, Xander thought.

When the last of the fans finally walked away, Sasha let out a long breath, her shoulders slumping as she released the tension she'd obviously been holding.

Xander strode over and met her gaze. "You okay?" he asked.

She nodded. "I'm fine. I was just hoping to fly under the radar here. I'm not all made up, not dressed to stand out." She shrugged, disappointment in her eyes. "Guess not."

He narrowed his gaze. Did she really not see how she stood out in a crowd? "You don't need all that artificial crap to be noticed." He glanced at the manager, who was waiting to escort them to their table, and nodded.

The man led them to a secluded corner and gestured for them to sit. "I'm sorry about the crowd," he said. "I was in the back on a call with a distributor or I would have handled things sooner."

Sasha graced him with a genuine smile. "Thank you so much. I'm sorry to bring chaos to your restaurant," she said.

He shook his head and waved a hand, dismissing her concern. "You can't buy this kind of publicity," he said, walking away and leaving them alone.

"Well. That wasn't how I planned for things to go." She picked up the napkin on the table, shook it out, and placed it on her lap. "Let's talk about something other than ... *that.*" That meaning her being swarmed by fans.

The server came over and Xander asked her to give them more time.

He would willingly change the subject except for a lingering question he couldn't ignore. "I have to ask. The fans, the autographs, the starring roles. It's everything you wanted and, let's face it, everything you were willing to risk us for. You have that now, yet you seem ... sad? Stressed?"

She drew a deep breath and, with one finger, circled the top of her water glass that was already on the table. "In order to explain, I need to go back. Are you sure you're ready for the conversation?" she asked, putting him on the spot.

Though he hadn't meant to bring up the discussion of their past, he understood they had no choice but to talk so he could put it behind him and work with her on the movie. It wasn't easy.

For almost a year, he'd thought he'd found the woman who would define his future. They'd broken up without real closure, and now he had to wrap things up in a public restaurant, of all places. But that was his fault for refusing to talk at his house, a decision he now attributed to the shock of seeing her again.

"I can handle it," he finally said, his shoulders stiff, his hands in fists in his lap.

She nodded. "Okay then." Drawing a deep breath, she started to speak. "When we got together, I was trying to make a name for myself in the industry, and the night we met exposed me to big names for the first time. I'd already had a supporting role in a movie that was due out, and I was poised, as my agent likes to say. Does that make sense?"

"It does. And I understood that." And he really had.

He'd been in town for everything that having a say in his first movie entailed. He'd rented a house for a year, testing whether or not he liked LA, and he'd tried to be open-minded. To put his time in Afghanistan and the occasional bouts of anxiety behind him. He was home in one piece, so were his buddies, and he wasn't going back. He'd been looking toward the future and thought that would include Sasha.

She tipped her head to the side. "I know you tried to be accepting of my running around on auditions, taking meetings, having to cancel plans we'd made." She swallowed hard and twisted a long strand of hair around her finger. A nervous gesture he remembered well.

"Yes. But what I didn't understand or accept was how you ended up in a relationship with another man *for show*"—he paused to emphasize the words with finger quotes—"or taking a limo and walking the red carpet with him because it looked good for the movie."

From the living room sofa, watching on his laptop, the entire situation hadn't looked fake to him. Not with her co-star Marcus Collins's hands all over her on the red carpet that Xander had offered to walk her down. Despite knowing the lights and crowds and yelling photographers would possibly trigger him, he'd volunteered. For her. She knew it would have been hard for him, but he'd been willing to *try*.

She leaned forward in her seat. "I explained that to you," she said, her soft gaze meeting his. "My agent wanted us to arrive together and give the audience what they wanted. What they assumed to be true."

And that truth had included Marcus's mouth on hers for every photographer to capture for posterity.

Xander had watched and waited for her to react, to stiffen in shock or discreetly move the dick's hand off her ass. Anything to prove to Xander she might suck up the situation for appearances but she was *his* and she'd take care of the bastard when the cameras weren't focused on her.

But when a reporter stopped the couple and asked about their status, Marcus had pulled Sasha closer and kissed her on the lips a second time, with his tongue. Then he'd turned to the camera with a grin and asked, "Does that answer your question?"

Sasha hadn't batted an eyelash at his actions or response.

Xander raised his eyebrows. "And the kisses?" He made sure to use the plural.

She briefly closed her eyes before meeting his gaze. "At the time, I thought I was doing what was best, but I was also *acting*. Doing my job in front of the cameras."

And she was damned good at it. Then and now. So what if he'd caught a movie or two of hers in the privacy of his home? Nobody had to know.

He braced his arms on the table. "We didn't break up over Marcus Collins. It was the culmination of many things, but the final straw was—"

"Paris," she said.

"Paris." He inclined his head. "You took that role

without giving me a heads-up first. We'd been living together almost a year. Don't you think I deserved at least a discussion before you decided you were going to be gone for months overseas?" He wouldn't have stopped her, but she should have offered reassurances about them.

"I—" she began.

He cut her off. "You weren't the least bit upset about it because you were so excited that your dreams were coming true." And though everything inside him had been ready to end things because he'd grown tired of barely being an afterthought, he knew he loved her. So he'd talked to his siblings, the people closest to him, and he'd decided to try one last time. "And I accepted Paris, too."

He'd gone on with his life in LA. Was available for the post-production process of his film and worked on an upcoming book in his free time. He'd tried to make things work with Sasha, but video calls, texting, and phone conversations were hard with the different time zones. She'd often been called away mid-sentence and he had been frustrated.

"It was a hard time," she admitted. "And it was complicated for me. I had a lot of pressure from my agent and my mother."

Her mother had never liked Xander, whether it was their age difference or the fact that he might derail

Sasha's career, it hadn't mattered. She'd always been a negative voice in her daughter's ear. It made sense that she'd both wanted and needed the approval of the parent who'd raised her and also encouraged her to pursue her dreams. Even if Annika had been trying to live vicariously through her daughter.

And yet, he'd understood. "I loved you, so I supported you."

She winced at his use of the past tense, but it was the truth. Those feelings were in the past.

She nodded, tears in her eyes. "I know you did. And I appreciated it."

Did she? He didn't want to be a dick and ask.

"But when those photos of you and yet another co-star surfaced…" He shook his head. Sasha and Corey Murphy had been spotted cozying up in a small café, sharing a booth, heads bent together in what looked like an intimate conversation. The photos went viral. And Xander had had enough.

He wasn't a jealous man but she'd pushed him to the brink. "At that point, I didn't care if the rumors and the photos showed the truth or not."

"They weren't," she said in a strong voice, and he actually believed her and acknowledged the point with a nod.

"But I also knew I couldn't live the Hollywood life. *Your* life."

She sighed but remained silent.

Xander had solid reasons for his feelings. He'd grown up with a father who'd been a serial cheater, and he'd resolved never to be that man or to accept it in his life, as his mother had. Plus, he'd already been fed up with LA. He'd been alone in a city and living a lifestyle he hated. The woman he loved had been halfway around the world, and there was nothing about their relationship that was sustainable. Not for him. Not when she'd allowed things to happen that would hurt him in order to get ahead.

Since they opened these old wounds, he might as well be one-hundred-percent honest with her. "I knew I'd always come third or fourth in your priorities. I just put an end to it before you did, by leaving."

She stiffened at the reminder. "Before I came back and over Facetime." She clasped her hands tightly on the table in front of her.

"I guess we both did what we thought was best at the time."

She jerked at his parallel use of her words and scowled at him.

"You still haven't explained why you're not flying high on your success now," he said.

The server returned to their table. "Are you ready to order?" she asked, politely.

"Can you give us another few minutes?" Xander

wanted this conversation over and done with, not to be revisited.

"Of course," the woman said.

Once she left, he met Sasha's gaze.

"I'm just tired," she said. "Not with acting. You have nothing to worry about when it comes to me playing Amanda. It's just some of the other things that go with the career that are draining me. It's been like a merry-go-round lately, going from one film to the next, one country to another." She lifted her shoulder and lowered it again. "But I know how lucky I am to have achieved so much so quickly. I'll just take a break after this movie and I'll be fine." Her gaze darted from his, and he had the distinct sense she wasn't telling him everything.

But she didn't owe him an explanation, and now he had a better understanding of ... nothing. He'd asked the question, hoping for insight into the woman he'd once loved, and he'd wound up being the one who rehashed the low points of their relationship. Once he'd started, he hadn't been able to stop, barely giving her a chance to talk.

He ran his hand over his head and, not for the first time, debated growing out his hair. At least he'd have something to pull on when shit went south.

He glanced at her. "I think we should arrange for a car to pick us up after we eat. Hopefully we can avoid fan craziness if someone posts you're here on social media."

"I already texted my assistant and she's taking care of it." A wry smile lifted her lips and she shrugged. "It's part of my life."

He nodded, hating that she lived this kind of life all the more.

When it came time to order, Sasha chose a chicken breast paillard, and Xander opted for a pizza with prosciutto, tomato, and mozzarella.

They changed the subject to the character of Amanda in his novel, spending the meal and their coffee discussing the strong woman he'd written to be Steele's new dynamic female lead. A woman who could stand up to the Marine, much more than his wife ever had, and one who would ultimately become a partner in his adventures. Sasha asked intriguing questions, forcing Xander to think about the character from an entirely different perspective.

The tension from earlier evaporated, and their old dynamic reappeared, in both the back-and-forth dialogue between them and in her joking and teasing to his more serious persona. Somehow, they meshed. He'd forgotten just how well. Despite the rehashing of history earlier, he relaxed as they talked and enjoyed their time together.

But now he stared at the woman in front of him,

seeing her in a new light. She possessed a fresh confidence in her abilities that came with experience, and she wasn't afraid to offer differing opinions on motivation and conflict, things she'd need to know in order to create and become Amanda. He found everything about her, from her intelligence to her gorgeous face with that pert nose and full lips, so fucking sexy. She'd matured in so many ways. Which made him realize just how young she really had been when they were together before.

"Why are you looking at me like that?" Sasha asked, eyes gleaming as they had since they'd stopped talking about the past and begun concentrating on the present.

He shook his head and pushed aside the coffee he'd been drinking. "I'm just impressed with your ability to get inside Amanda's head. It's like you're understanding what I was thinking when I wrote her, only on a deeper level."

She beamed at his compliment, her cheeks flushed pink. "I really liked her when I read the book, and I love discussing all aspects of a character I'm going to play."

"Did you get enough information from me?" he asked.

She studied him intently before answering. "For now," she said, a teasing smile on her face.

The server placed the check on the table, and Xander immediately nabbed the bill and put his credit card inside. She left a few mints on the table, and while they waited for the check, Sasha popped one into her mouth. Xander did the same.

Once he signed and paid, he led her out through the back entrance hoping to avoid any fan encounters. Without thinking, his hand came to rest on her lower back, and his palm came in contact with bare skin.

His entire being reacted to the feel of soft female flesh. Of *Sasha's* flesh. Even his dick, which he'd kept under control during dinner, rose up and made an appearance.

Before he could deal with his body's reaction, the flash of camera lights went off and people surrounded them, all trying to get a picture of Sasha and, Xander was sure, the man with her so they could make up lies about their relationship. So much for avoiding the fans.

One man in particular grabbed her arm and tried to pull her away. Xander already had a hand on her back and managed to slide his arm around her waist and yank her tight against him. Rushing, he pushed through the crowd, all the while fighting his racing heart. Sweat covered his body but he managed to remain in the present. He always did. Unless he heard a loud sound that reminded him of Afghanistan, he'd be able to hold on to reality. Or so the therapist he'd seen when he'd come home had told him.

Fear for her filled him much more than any kind of panic for himself, because he'd heard stories of crazed fans lunging for famous targets and doing damage.

Xander caught sight of a man in a suit standing ready by the back door of a dark sedan.

"Miss Kingston," he said, pulling open the door as they reached him.

Xander pushed her inside before joining her. The driver slammed the door shut and a few moments later, he was behind the wheel, driving them away from the crowd.

Chapter Four

ONCE IN THE back seat of the car, Sasha leaned back, her heart pounding in her chest. Being accosted by fans as well as photographers was a scary thing, and she tried hard not to be noticed but since becoming a household name, if she was spotted, she reacted accordingly, taking her safety seriously. In LA she grudgingly used security, but she'd really thought nobody would look for her in New York before filming started. She'd been so stupid to think she could go out and not be recognized.

Thank God Xander had pulled her against him and rushed for the car.

Xander.

She opened her eyes to find him staring at her, his jaw tight, a muscle throbbing in his temple. She knew in that instant all the progress they'd made over the meal had dispersed with the crowd.

"Why the hell don't you have a bodyguard?" he asked.

She blew out a long breath. "Because I don't want to live like that."

He frowned at her reply. "That's a case of *be careful what you wish for*," he muttered, more than a hint of frustration in his tone.

"What's that supposed to mean?"

He turned toward her. "Do I really need to spell it out for you? You have everything you dreamed of. Now you need to acknowledge it and take care of yourself."

She glared at him. "Wow, that's patronizing."

His serious gaze bore into hers and he grasped her shoulders. "It's common sense! Do you realize what could have happened if that guy had grabbed you and I hadn't been there?"

His concern for her was surprising given the distance he'd been keeping. And she didn't want to consider the scenario he was talking about because he was right. She'd read about celebrities accosted and hurt by crazy fans.

"I'm *fine*," she assured him as well as herself.

"But what if you weren't?" Fire blazed in his blue eyes as his grip on her tightened.

He wasn't hurting her but his intensity was extreme. And she knew why. Given his military history and the IED blast that had taken him out of commission, he had an overprotective streak for those he cared about. She didn't delude herself that she was one of those people. Not anymore. But the crush of people and the overeager male fan had triggered him.

She reached up and touched her hand to his cheek, feeling the softness of his beard for the first time. "We're both safe," she said softly.

His gaze fell to her lips, and his eyes darkened in a way she recognized. Her heart skipped a beat, and her stomach flipped as awareness settled between them. She leaned in, all the while wondering what she was doing. She'd barely survived losing him the first time. Not that he knew how she'd fallen apart, and she felt certain he'd never believe her if she told him. Because he'd been right. She *had* put her career front and center.

But with his mouth so close to hers, she couldn't worry about the past and kissed him before he could change his mind.

He stilled at the touch of her lips to his, and her breath caught as she waited for him to pull away.

He didn't.

Instead, he turned her against the back seat of the car and took charge, clearly needing to feel in control of himself, of her, and of life in general. One hand cupped her face, his thumb brushing her cheek while his mouth devoured, his tongue sliding back and forth, tangling with hers.

She'd missed him. Missed this and drowned in his familiar scent and taste. His beard scratched her face and she didn't care. The sensation aroused her, and she wanted so much more than a kiss in the back seat of a car. But she'd take what she could get and threaded her fingers through his short hair, lightly scratching his scalp and getting a harsh groan in reply.

And then they were jolted when the vehicle came to a stop and the driver spoke. "We're here."

"Shit." Xander jerked himself off her, as if the driver's words brought reality crashing back.

She didn't have to look at him to know he regretted the kiss. Her lips still tingled from the brush of his beard; she still tasted his minty flavor in her mouth. And her body would continue to remind her of what she'd lost. He'd been so amped up from escaping the crowd, he'd forgotten how he really felt about her.

He exited the car first. She slid across the seat and stepped out, accepting the hand he offered. Xander Kingston was nothing if not a gentleman.

Then he slammed the door shut and she forced herself to meet his gaze. His closed-off expression told her all she needed to know, and she had no intention of prolonging the inevitable.

"Thanks for dinner and the information about Amanda. I'll see you on set," she said, turning to go.

"Wait." He touched her shoulder, and she glanced back. "I'll walk you to your room."

She had no desire for a long goodbye. "Thanks but

I'll be okay."

He raised an eyebrow. "You hoped for the same thing when we left the restaurant. Humor me," he said, gesturing for her to go first.

She knew better than to argue, and they headed inside the hotel, walking through the lobby. They reached the elevators, and he stood beside her as she pressed the up button.

She glanced at him. "I'm sure I can get to my room without a problem."

The doors opened and he stepped inside along with her, subjecting her to his heady body heat and scent in the enclosed space. With a deliberately loud sigh, she pulled her keycard from her purse and watched the floor numbers go upward, waiting in silence while wishing this awkwardness would end.

She had nothing to say and clearly he didn't either. His one-word curse earlier had been enough.

The elevator stopped, the doors opened, and she strode to her room. She opened the door, planning to turn and tell him to leave, but the sound of familiar voices distracted her.

In the suite sat Cassidy with Rebecca and Dina Addams, her publicist, who was located in LA but had come to the city for meetings this coming week.

"What's wrong? What is everyone doing here?" Sasha entered the room and Xander stepped in behind her.

"It's about time you got back! Since when don't you check your phone?" Rebecca asked.

"I… We were busy talking. What's going on?" Sasha glanced at her team.

Rebecca, a dedicated career woman at sixty years old, still looked closer to fifty. She wore her hair in a short bob and was the epitome of New York chic. Dina was in her early forties, dressed like she was twenty-five, and handled some of the most famous people in Hollywood.

"Shut the door," Dina said.

Xander immediately let go and the door closed behind him.

Whatever was going on, Sasha didn't want him as an audience and turned his way. "As you can see, I'm here and I'm safe. You can go now."

His scowl deepened and Dina spoke. "Let him stay. He'll be on set. He should know what's going on."

"What *is* going on? Is someone going to tell me?" Sasha strode over to the cocktail table by the sofa and put her purse down before leveling her team, one by one, with a hard stare.

Cassidy looked the most worried.

"Cass?"

Her friend sighed. "I ordered dinner, and while I

was waiting, I took a shower. When I came out, a note had been slipped under the door. I thought it was a bill they'd put for you to look over even though we weren't checking out soon." She twisted her hands in front of her.

"It wasn't?" This came from Xander.

Sasha had almost forgotten he was there. *Almost.*

"No, it wasn't." Dina, who stood by the window, stepped in closer. "You received a note," she said to Sasha.

"Can I see?"

The other women looked at each other before Dina pulled a sealed plastic bag from her tote. "Just preserving evidence as best I can," she said.

"Evidence?" Sasha took the bag and looked at the paper with the words *You're Mine* on the page. Each letter, individually cut out and pasted on the paper, had a different computer font.

"Jesus Christ," Xander said from behind her, his big body vibrating with anger.

"Someone sent this to me?" she asked, unease rippling through her.

"Yes," Dina said.

Sasha blew out a long breath, trying to be rational. "Okay, well, we all know celebrities get notes from obsessed fans all the time. It doesn't mean–"

"It means someone reached your floor and got as

far as your door. Which is why I said you need security," Xander all but growled in her ear.

"We'll get to that," Rebecca said.

Dina cleared her throat. "Unfortunately, this isn't the first note you've gotten that has this … possessive tone."

Sasha's mail was sent through Dina's agency. They vetted each piece and forwarded on to Cassidy what was important. It helped keep both Sasha's and Cassidy's life manageable and the crazies at a distance.

"How many more notes has she gotten?" Xander stepped around Sasha and pulled the bag out of Dina's hand.

The publicist shifted from foot to foot in her expensive heels. "We run her social media accounts, and I have someone pulling the messages and actual fan snail mail as we speak. But quite a few."

Anger and concern rushed through Sasha. She paid these people to handle things and report back to her. If they didn't, how could she know she was safe? "Why wasn't I told about them?"

"For the reason you just mentioned. Our clients get these kinds of emails, snail mail, and direct messages often," Dina said. "The only time we bring them to their attention is if the contents seem dangerous or it escalates. Otherwise, there would be no point in us handling things for you."

Her reasoning made sense but Sasha wasn't completely satisfied.

"I don't like this," Xander muttered. "Not after today."

"What happened today?" It sounded like all three women asked the same question at once.

Xander folded his arms across his broad chest. "Someone recognized her, which led to autographs and photos. After we ate dinner, she was surrounded on her way out of the restaurant. A guy grabbed her and tried to pull her away."

"Xander wrapped an arm around me and we made it to the car that Cassidy arranged for us." Sasha hadn't been as freaked out by the incident as he had, mostly because she'd been in those situations before. But now? "Do you think it's the same person? The guy who grabbed me and the one who left the note?"

"Serafina is within walking distance," he said of the restaurant. "It could be the same person. Or it could be two different people." He'd begun pacing back and forth in the suite.

Although the room normally felt big, with his long strides and large build, the area seemed to shrink, and she grew more aware of him. It didn't matter that there were three others in the room. Xander took up all her oxygen.

"Either way, I don't like this." He turned to face

her. "I'm calling a friend of mine who runs a body-guard business. Alpha Security is the best and I'm bringing them in," he said.

"I—" she began.

"Not up for argument." Xander had an obstinate expression on his face as he interrupted her and his determined gaze met hers.

She shrugged. "I was just going to say I have a company on retainer. I don't plan on being stupid with my safety."

Dina cleared her throat. "Your firm in LA is solid," she said. "A lot of my clients use them."

Xander glared at her. "Alpha is excellent and they're local. Dash uses them, and if they're good enough for the Original Kings, I feel comfortable hiring them for Sasha."

"*You* feel comfortable? Why are we considering your feelings? And why is everyone talking around me instead of *to* me?" Sasha glared at Xander, the person she was most upset with, the memory of his reaction to their kiss still lingering along with the hurt she felt at his rejection.

"Excuse us a minute," she said to everyone else in the room before grabbing his hand and pulling him into the bedroom, slamming the door shut behind them.

★　★　★

XANDER KNEW HE was in trouble. He let Sasha drag him into the adjoining bedroom and waited for her to explode at his high-handed behavior. Not that he cared. There was no way he was going to turn her safety over to anyone but the best.

She faced him, hands on her hips. "What are you doing?"

"Making sure you're protected. Do you think I'm going to let the PR firm who didn't tell you about potential stalker issues handle your safety?" he asked.

Her beautiful blue eyes opened wide. "How about you let *me* handle it? God knows I've been capable of taking care of myself since you left me."

He narrowed his gaze. "I'd say you checked out of the relationship first, but that's not the point."

He didn't want to get into a petty fight about the past when he needed to focus on the present. She'd been threatened by a stalker, and he intended to take care of her—without allowing himself to dig into the reasons why he cared so much. From the moment that crazy fan had grabbed her and tried pulling her away, a switch had flipped inside him and his protector instincts had kicked in.

And since she looked about to launch into an argument again, he cut her off. "I can make one call and have someone by your side in under an hour. Are you going to argue?"

"Fine."

"Good." He pulled his cell out of his pocket and got his brother on the phone. "Dash, I need a favor."

"Talk to me."

Xander heard music playing in the background. "Your security people. I need someone immediately for Sasha. She's at the Gansevoort, but I'm bringing her to my place, where it's quiet and we can see a stranger coming. Can you get me someone to protect her?"

"You're bringing me where?" Sasha's voice echoed in the room. Her pouty lips parted in shock, and Xander prepared himself for another fight.

On the other end of the call, his brother was silent and Xander knew why. It was only a matter of time before–

"What the fuck are you doing?" Dash asked. "Didn't she hurt you enough the first time?"

"That's not what this is about. Can you help me out or not?" Xander asked.

Xander glanced at Sasha, who was tapping her foot, her anxiety and fury obvious. He didn't blame her. No more than he faulted his sibling for worrying about him. Xander would do the same if the situation were reversed.

"On it, bro, but I hope you know what you're do-ing. Someone from Alpha will be in touch soon."

"Thanks." Xander disconnected the call.

"I'm not staying with you. That's what a bodyguard is for," Sasha said.

"That may be true but this is Manhattan. It's crowded. Look how easily that guy got close to you today. And someone managed to reach your floor and slip a note under your door. What if the man shows up with a room service cart?"

She blinked at him. "Have you been watching too much television?" she asked, but she was nibbling on her bottom lip, which told him she was thinking about what he'd said.

So he went in for the kill. "I live on secluded property, I have a big dog, and the nearest house is my brother's. If anyone comes around, we'll see them coming. No crowds."

"No room service carts?" Her lips twitched in a grin she tried to hide.

He couldn't help but laugh. "Wiseass."

"What about Cassidy?"

He gave the question some thought. "I think she's safe in the city though I'd probably move her to a new hotel and put a guard on her. Just to be safe."

"It's just for the weekend, right? Because we're back in the city for filming on Monday," Sasha said.

He shoved his hands into his pants pockets. "For now, yes. It's for this weekend. We'll discuss what happens next on Sunday."

She eyed him warily but remained quiet, obviously not ready to know what he had in mind.

His mouth quirked and he suppressed a smile. He still needed to come to terms with the fact that he planned to keep her by his side for the duration of her time in New York. All through filming.

"Does that mean you're coming home with me?" He told himself he just wanted to keep her safe and all his reasons made perfect sense. So why was his heart pounding hard in his chest as he waited for her to answer? And why couldn't he get that kiss, one he'd only indulged in after a panicked moment, out of his head?

She stared at him as if she'd find the answers in his expression before finally nodding. "I'll come."

He blew out a breath, relieved.

They headed back into the suite, and she got to work convincing her team they had a handle on things. Her agent and publicist left, promising to keep in close contact. Cassidy agreed to move hotels, and Sasha packed up her things. They dropped her personal assistant off at a new hotel and headed uptown, where they picked up Bella at his apartment. He hooked his dog up to her safety harness in the back of his SUV, and they started their trip to his Hamptons home.

Sasha was quiet as they drove. The satellite radio

station played classic rock, and her silence continued for the duration of the trip. Assuming she was preoccupied with the sudden upheaval in her life and the stalker threat, he figured he'd get her talking tomorrow.

At close to ten p.m., Xander finally pulled into his driveway. It was dark, but the automatic lights turned on at his approach, and a car was idling in his extra parking spot.

"Probably your security," he said.

Sasha nodded. "Yes. I just wish there wasn't a need."

The urge to pull her into his arms and reassure her was strong. Incredibly so. No sooner had he found out she was in danger than the anger he felt toward her had begun to soften.

Suddenly he was able to put emotion aside and think clearly about their past. She'd been all of twenty when they were together last, and it was hard to imagine she'd had a good grasp on life or relationships at that age. And he'd definitely expected a lot of her at a time when everything around her had been changing fast.

Maybe they both shared responsibility for how things ended.

But just because he was coming closer to forgiving her and providing her with a secure place to stay now didn't mean he'd forgotten how badly she'd hurt him. Or the fact that their lives could never mesh. But he couldn't deny the pull she exerted over him, either.

"Xander, what's wrong?" Sasha put a hand on his arm, shaking him out of his thoughts.

He shook his head. "Everything's fine. I was just thinking." He opened the SUV door, climbed out, and Sasha did the same. She met him on his side as he unhooked Bella and let her off the leash. The dog quickly ran to do her thing on the grass.

A large man wearing jeans and a dark sport jacket stepped out of his vehicle. With his overall don't-fuck-with-me appearance, he had personal security stamped all over him.

He joined them and spoke immediately. "Jared Wilson of Alpha Security," he said. "And you're Sasha Keaton."

Smiling, she shook his hand and then he turned to Xander. "And you're Dash's brother."

Xander nodded. "Xander Kingston."

"I see the resemblance," Jared said.

"You've worked for Dash?" Xander asked as he strode behind the SUV and raised the back with the push of a button.

Jared shook his head. "Others on my team have, but he's out back in the pool with the rest of the band."

"At this hour?" Xander groaned and pulled first one then another of Sasha's suitcases out of the trunk. "I'll talk to him about just showing up while we're on guard."

"Xander, no." Sasha put her hand on his arm, and damned if it didn't feel good. "Your brother should be able to come over any time he wants."

He met her gaze. "You do realize that my brother lives a mile down the road, has his own house, his own pool, and just comes here to drive me crazy?" Xander loved the bastard, but he really didn't understand personal space.

And Xander had no doubt that Dash had made it over here in time to see Sasha. Whether he behaved or not was anyone's guess, but he'd better not cross a line. No matter Xander's history with his ex, she wasn't here so Dash could make her uncomfortable.

"As long as I know who's allowed in and out, we're fine," Jared said. "I spoke to your publicity team, Ms. Keaton."

"Sasha, please."

He inclined his head. "They're going to forward our tech guy the letters you received. In the meantime, given the fact that someone's been close to you twice now, I'll be switching off shifts with Tate Shaw. You'll have someone on alert twenty-four seven."

"Thank you," she said, visibly relieved.

"Sasha, why don't you go inside." Xander handed her the keys. If Dash was here, the alarm was already unset. "I just want to talk to Jared for a few minutes."

She nodded, grabbed the handle on her smaller bag, and rolled it toward the house.

As soon as she was out of earshot, Xander turned to Sasha's new personal security. "My property already has cameras because, as you see, Dash comes and goes at random times," he said of his famous brother. "But can your people do a thorough check and upgrade whatever you feel is necessary?"

Jared nodded. "Got it."

"We're only going to be out east for the weekend, and then we'll be in Manhattan for filming, but we'll be back on weekends." Upgrading his security system was smart, regardless of how long Sasha would be here.

Jared nodded. "No problem. I'll talk to Dan," he said of the man in charge of the agency. "Where will you be staying in the city?"

"My apartment." Not that Sasha was aware of his plans, but he figured he'd be able to talk her into it the same way he'd done today. "The building has a concierge at the front desk, and you can cover outside my door in case someone gets past them. And you'll take us back and forth to the set."

"Consider it done," Jared said.

They discussed a few more details and shook hands before Xander headed inside.

SASHA STEPPED INTO Xander's house. At least she'd been here once before and was somewhat familiar with the layout. The pool was out back, and she could hear the sounds of men's voices from outside. The band. When Xander had lived in LA, his family had taken turns coming to visit, and Dash had only recently been signed by his label. Sasha liked their music and had always gotten along with Dash Kingston, but she had no idea what kind of greeting she was in for tonight.

Exhaustion filled her as she pulled her bag with her toiletries and cosmetics into the main room and set it out of the way. She'd been on autopilot since agreeing to stay here and had only said yes because Xander had made such a valid point about his house being secluded. And she knew Bella would bark at the sound of intruders. Sasha didn't know where she'd stay when they had to go back to the city for filming, but she was too tired to think about it tonight.

While she waited for Xander, she called her manager and made sure *she* was the one paying the Alpha Security bill. As she disconnected her call, she got the sense she was being watched.

She turned to find Dash Kingston standing in the

arched entry between the family room and the kitchen. His hair was damp and both darker and longer than Xander's. He wore bathing trunks and a tee shirt, and though he had the Kingston good looks, where Xander was well-built, Dash was leaner. But she recalled him working out and possessing tight abs his female fans loved. He just wasn't bulked up like his brother. And it was Xander who made Sasha's heart soar.

Just like Xander, Dash had perfected that pissed-off scowl. "At least you're not after him for his money." Apparently Dash had heard her side of the call with her manager.

She knew the depth of this family's protective nature and did her best not to take his attitude personally. She'd always envied him having siblings who were so close.

"So that begs the question," Dash continued, "why are you here?" He folded his strong arms across his chest.

She wouldn't let him intimidate her. "You know why. I needed protection, and your brother insisted I'd be safer here than in the city. And it's nice to see you, too, Dash."

He studied her for a long moment, and she had no idea if she passed his inspection. "I liked you, Sasha, but you hurt my brother once. I hope you're not here to do more damage."

"Dash, back off," Xander said on what sounded like a growl.

She hadn't heard him come in.

"Sasha's an invited guest." He pulled her last piece of luggage behind him and set it next to her other suitcase. "Which is more than I can say for you and the band."

"Hey, that's not true. I have an open invite. Tell her," Dash said with a pout she'd bet the ladies adored, and Sasha did her best not to laugh out loud at the banter she remembered.

"Seriously, why aren't you at *your* pool?" Xander asked.

Dash lost the lighthearted expression. "We're having some disagreements within the band and we thought…"

"A change of scenery would help," both men said at the same time and Dash grinned again. "See? You get it."

Xander rolled his eyes. "Gather the guys and go home."

"They're eating a late dinner." Playfulness once again danced in Dash's eyes, but he caught Xander's glare. "We didn't raid your fridge. We ordered in. Well, we might have taken drinks from you. But the pizza was on us."

Dash turned and walked back through the kitchen, and she heard the sliding glass door open. "Time for you guys to pack it up and go home!" he yelled at the band.

"You're going with them," Xander called out to his brother, then met Sasha's gaze, an amused smile pulling at his sexy mouth.

A mouth she'd kissed earlier. At the reminder, she slid her tongue over her bottom lip, and his gaze tracked the movement.

He cleared his throat. "Let me show you to your room."

They each took a suitcase, and she followed him to the front of the house, where he paused.

"What's wrong?" she asked.

Turning, he ran a hand over his beard. "The master is this way." He pointed to the hallway on the right. "There's a second bedroom with a bathroom in the hall."

She swallowed hard. "Okay."

"That way," he said, pointing left, "there are three other bedrooms and two bathrooms. You'd have more privacy there."

"I hear a *but*?" she asked, because this was not a decision she wanted to make. She'd go where he sent her. It was his house and his decision because he needed to be comfortable in his own home.

"But I'd feel better knowing you were close by." He looked as if the admission cost him something, but she let out a relieved breath.

"Me, too," she admitted softly. She was totally freaked out by that note.

You're Mine. Who the hell would stake a claim on her that way? Knowing Xander was a few steps away made her feel even better than being aware of the bodyguard outside.

He reached out a hand and stroked her cheek. "Nobody's going to get near you," he said gruffly. "Now let me show you your room. After I'm sure Dash and the guys are gone, I'll teach you how to set and unset the alarm."

She nodded. "Sounds good."

He led her to the bedroom across the hall from the master and pulled her bag inside. "Want me to put the heavy one on the bed so you can unpack?"

"Sure."

He lifted the heavy suitcase and placed it on the blanket at the end of the comforter. "If you need anything, let me know."

She watched him head for the door, but before he stepped out, she called his name.

He turned, eyebrows raised.

"I just wanted to say thank you for taking care of me. Given our past, you helping me means a lot."

He treated her to a nod and walked out, leaving her to unpack and get comfortable in his house, across from his bedroom.

Chapter Five

X ANDER SLEPT WELL knowing Sasha was safe and across the hall, but he woke up with morning wood. He pressed his hand against the sheet, groaning at how fucking hard he was. Closing his eyes, he slipped his hand beneath and gave a few healthy tugs of his dick before kicking off the comforter and rising to a sitting position. He wasn't going to make himself come with Sasha's name on his lips when the real woman was a few steps away.

His time would be better spent getting his head on straight and deciding what he wanted from her while they were under the same roof. A good, long run would help him decide. Many of his life choices were made while pounding the pavement.

He walked out of his room, Bella trotting beside him. The door across from his was still closed. He let the dog out back and returned to the bedroom to get ready. He had his family coming later this afternoon, which meant he needed to check in with the store owner who would be delivering everything he'd ordered during the week. Something he could do while he was in town.

After he dressed, he turned on his phone and chose the playlist he wanted for today. He walked outside and nodded at Jared, who was still on duty. If Sasha hadn't had someone watching over her, Xander would never have left her alone.

He took off at a jog, Bella by his side. His playlist had an eclectic list of songs from Bruce Springsteen and Eminem to Tom Petty, Kanye West, and the Rolling Stones. For a while, he got lost in the rhythm and the sound and feel of his feet smacking the street.

As he and Bella neared town, Xander slowed his pace, wiping his forehead with the bottom of his shirt. He stopped at a store that kept a water bowl outside for pets and let Bella take a drink.

"Good girl," he said, giving her fur a rub.

Taking Bella with him because stores in town were dog friendly, he walked inside and confirmed an afternoon delivery of grilling burgers, hotdogs, buns, and other things for his family to enjoy. He bought himself water with the money tucked into his pocket and took a long drink before tossing the bottle into a recycling basket and heading home at a slower jog.

The minute his feet found their rhythm again, he let himself think about Sasha and what he wanted from her. That answer was easy. He wanted her in his bed, his hands on her soft body, his cock buried deep inside her. Admitting that, he nearly tripped, caught himself, and accepted what he already knew. He wouldn't be satisfied unless he had Sasha again. Deep down, he'd known the truth since her return, more so since realizing she'd been threatened and his protective feelings had shown up.

He didn't think they had another chance at a future. He already knew that was impossible. He'd had firsthand proof that her life was everything he didn't want. But he definitely needed to bury himself inside her once more.

He glanced at Bella, who kept pace beside him as they ran, passing other houses set back from the beach and admiring the sun as it shone brightly above him. Though he appreciated the scenery, his thoughts were on the woman staying with him for the next few weeks.

He couldn't keep treating her like she was the enemy or continue to hold her at arm's length. He already knew, when she was finished filming, she'd return to Los Angeles and her busy life, and he'd go back to writing and being at peace here at home. But before either of those things happened, they could enjoy each other while she was in town. And he'd just have to let her go when her time here was over.

SASHA WOKE UP in a strange bed. Nothing new to her. She was used to hotels and travel, but as soon as her mind started to function, she remembered she was in Xander's house because she needed protection from a stalker. No wonder she'd crashed hard last night. She'd been exhausted from a long day.

Yesterday had been tough and she needed to remain calm. She had a bodyguard now and was staying somewhere safe where she could unwind and work on the part she'd be playing in the movie. And try not to think about the danger while letting the professionals do their job.

The first thing she did was call Cassidy and check in.

Cass picked up after the second ring. "Hey! I hoped you would call soon. How are you doing?"

Sasha let out a long breath, relieved to be talking to her friend. "I'm okay. It's quiet here and the security guy was waiting when we got in last night. How about you?"

"The hotel's nice and so is my bodyguard. Her name is Ava Talbott and she's on top of things here. But still, I don't think I need protection."

Sasha rolled her eyes. "You do. What if the stalker thinks I'm staying with you but hiding out? Then you're in danger, too."

"Fine. And thank you for taking care of me. Now

what can I do for you?"

Sasha glanced up at the ceiling, thinking about her upcoming itinerary. "Confirm this week's schedule and check in with Dina. Make sure her firm sends whatever letters and mail they've been keeping from us over to the new security team."

"On it," Cassidy said.

"And if you need me, don't hesitate to call."

"I will." She paused. "How are things going with Xander?"

Sasha bit down on the inside of her cheek. "Awkward and uncomfortable." But she was hoping she could break through his reserve.

"I'm sure you'll charm him soon enough," Cassidy said. "Yell if you need a pep talk, okay?"

Sasha laughed. "Will do." She said goodbye and disconnected the call.

It was time to tackle the day … and the man who was helping her. After a refreshing shower, she chose an easy sundress, pulled her hair into a damp, messy bun, and headed to see what she could find for breakfast. The door to Xander's room was closed, and she made her way to the kitchen, Bella coming up to her, seemingly out of nowhere.

Sasha bent down to pet her soft head. "Hey, girl. Where do you sleep at night?" Did she have her own doggie bed somewhere or did she share the mattress with her dad? She remembered Xander in bed at night and wondered if he still slept naked.

She shook her head before she could let her mind travel further down that road. Rising, she walked through the house, the dog trotting by her side.

She entered the oversized kitchen to find the man she'd been thinking about standing by the stove. With his damp hair, he appeared freshly showered. He wore a pair of black sweats and an Original Kings faded tee shirt that accentuated the muscles in his forearms. And he had his sexy black glasses on his face, which told her his eyes were bothering him this morning. She wished he didn't have to deal with his head injury, but she did love looking at him with those frames.

He must have sensed her presence, because he glanced over before he flipped an omelet in the frying pan, using a spatula.

"Morning, sunshine."

She blinked at his use of the old nickname he had for her. One she'd pushed out of her mind, thinking she'd never hear him call her that again. But here he was, not only using it but he sounded different. His voice held a warmth and lightness he hadn't used around her since her return.

She told herself not to read too much into it. "Good morning." She walked up beside him and glanced down. "A vegetable omelet. It smells good."

"I'm glad because I'm making two."

"Thanks. Is your head bothering you?" She reached out to stroke his forehead and jerked her hand back, hoping he hadn't realized her intent.

The warmth in his gaze told her he was on to her. "I couldn't sleep and worked late last night. My eyes are strained and I have a slight headache." He shrugged. "The glasses help. You remember?" he asked, obviously surprised.

She smiled. "I do." She recalled a lot about him. But she was trying to give him space until he came around. "Did you already go for a run?" Another thing she recalled. He'd always taken a morning jog, and after seeing him with Bella the first day, she assumed he hadn't changed his routine.

"Yeah. I was also up early and jogging clears my head." He slid the spatula under the omelet, lifted it, and slipped it onto a plate before getting to work on another one he had already mixed and ready to go.

A few minutes later, she was sitting across from him, drinking a cup of coffee, and digging into a fabulous breakfast.

"How did you sleep?" he asked.

"Very well, actually. I was exhausted. And the bed in that room is very comfortable."

"Good. I'd hate for you to be miserable here." He winked, causing her stomach to flutter, and then he took a sip of his coffee.

She narrowed her gaze, noting she wasn't wrong. He was much more chill and relaxed, and she couldn't help but wonder what had changed between them, at least on his end. But it wasn't like she could ask him, *hey, so why don't you hate me this morning? Where's that barrier you've had up since I arrived?*

"So, what do you have planned for today?" she asked instead.

"Well … my family's coming this afternoon for a barbeque. We switch off houses and normally do it on Sundays, but today was easier for me since the movie starts filming on Monday…" His voice trailed off, no doubt as he caught her expression.

Somewhere between shocked and horrified would cover it, she thought.

"What's wrong?" he asked.

He was such a man. "Considering how Dash reacted to me being here, do you really think I'm ready to see them again all at one time?" She could only imagine how his mother and sister would react. Not to mention his new half sister. She shuddered at the thought of being frozen out by the women in his family.

His expression softened and he reached out, placing his big hand over hers. "I called them this morning. They've all been given a heads-up and warned not to act like Dash did. And if you'd like, why don't you invite your friend Cassidy? I'm sure that will help make you feel more comfortable."

She blinked in surprise. "Maybe you're not such a typical guy after all. That was ... nice."

He cocked an eyebrow. "I can be nice," he muttered.

"Not recently. I mean, if we're being honest, not until today. Unless you count last night's order for me to pack up and come stay here. But like I said, that was a command."

Her lips twitched as she teased him, her entire body relaxing now that she knew nobody would actually confront her. And the fact that he'd thought ahead and had her back? Surprising and gratifying at the same time.

This was not the man who'd greeted her a few days ago or who'd awkwardly told her to choose a room last night. "What changed?" she asked.

"What?" He removed his hand and picked up his mug of coffee.

"You're being ... kind to me. Why all of a sudden?" She couldn't hold in the question.

He ran a hand over his beard in a move she'd quickly come to like, the same way she now appreciated the feel his facial hair on her face when he'd kissed her. The thought had her squirming in her seat.

"For one thing, we need to coexist under the same roof," he said, taking her question seriously.

"And for another?" Because it was clear he had more on his mind.

"I've been doing some thinking." Those intense blue eyes stared at her.

"About?"

"Us."

Her mouth parted in shock. Closing it again, she waited for him to continue. Meanwhile, her heart had begun pounding rapidly in her chest.

He stood up and pulled his chair closer to hers. "We can agree the chemistry is still there between us, yes?"

Xander, the man who'd wanted to keep his distance, was suddenly so close she found it hard to think clearly. Still, she managed to nod even as she wondered what point he was trying to make.

"I still want you," he said, his knuckles gliding over her cheek in a gesture that was both gentle and sexy and caused a rush of warmth between her thighs.

She drew a deep breath and inhaled the masculine scent that was pure Xander.

"This is where you say, *I want you, too*," he told her, a confident tilt lifting his lips.

She blinked, certain she'd stepped into an alternate universe where they'd never broken up and he'd pick her up and carry her to bed. "But…"

He slid a finger over her parted mouth. "First, tell me if we're on the same page," he said in a gruff voice.

"Desire doesn't change the past," she said. "Or the future. Or our issues." One of them had to think clearly. "I don't understand how you're suddenly past it all?"

He shrugged. "I wouldn't say I'm past it. But I am pragmatic. At least now I am. Last time we were together, I expected more from you than you could give. This time I know what's possible and what isn't. I know we can be together while you're here filming and part ways when it's time for you to leave. Except this time, we'll be friends when things end."

Friends. Part ways.

His words made perfect sense given the differences between their lifestyles, careers, and the fact that she lived across the country. So why the painful churning in her stomach and disappointment that settled in her chest? She pushed aside those feelings and focused on the present and the things she could control.

"Well?" he asked.

She leaned closer. "I want you, too," she said, staring into eyes that darkened behind the glasses.

She lifted the frames and slid them off his face, placing them on the table. Now she could look into his gorgeous gaze that was deepening with every second that passed.

Taking her off guard, he reached out and pulled her onto his lap, so she straddled his strong thighs. There was only soft material between her sex and his thick erection, and she couldn't contain the moan that escaped at the feel of him exactly where she needed pressure the most.

He gripped the back of her neck and drew her close until his mouth met hers. Desire swept through her, and she clenched her thighs around him, letting the brief wave of sensation wash over her. She swirled her tongue around his, and his mouth glided over hers, taking, demanding. Certain. Because this time he'd thought things through. He knew what he wanted and he was showing her.

It. Was. Glorious.

He nipped at her bottom lip and she rocked her hips, creating the friction her body needed. His fingers combed through her hair, and he pulled off the scrunchie, tossing it onto the floor. Her damp hair tumbled over her shoulders, and he wound the long strands around his hand, tugging until she tilted her head, giving him deeper access.

"Fuck, you taste good," he said, his thumb running over the pulse point in her neck, a move he followed with his tongue gliding over her skin.

Desire rippled through her, her underwear slick and wet. She grabbed the hem of his shirt and slipped her hands beneath, settling her palms on his muscular chest. "You feel good," she murmured into his mouth.

"So do you. I don't know where to touch first. Here?" The pad of his thumb slid over her bottom lip. "Or here?" He slipped one hand beneath her dress and held her waist in his hand. "Or here?" His talented fingers eased downward until his palm cupped her sex in his large hand.

"Hey, kids! I'm here to help set up for the barbeque… Oh, shit. Sorry!" Dash's voice interrupted them and Sasha broke the kiss.

She jerked herself away from Xander, and only his strong arms kept her from falling backward on her butt.

"Goddammit, I'm taking back your key," Xander muttered.

He helped her to her feet, his hands remaining on her waist until he was sure she was steady. She gave him a nod and stepped back, aware her cheeks were burning and flushed as she turned to face his brother.

"I didn't mean to interrupt." Dash spread his hands in front of him. "Sorry?"

Xander rolled his eyes. "Have you ever heard of using the doorbell? Better yet, text or call before you just show up next time?"

"The band is arguing again," Dash said, and Sasha realized he had serious issues going on with his band.

He obviously wanted to talk to Xander, and she needed to make herself scarce. Being alone would give her time to process what was happening between her and Xander. To decide how far she was willing to take things between them knowing for certain how things would end.

"Umm, I'm going to let you two talk. I can help you prepare for the barbeque, too. Let me know what I can do. I'll be in my room going over the script," she said.

"Are you sure?" Xander asked, longing and desire still in his eyes. "You don't need to go."

She glanced at Dash and shook her head. "Yes, I do."

Dash shot her a grateful glance, and she hoped he'd put his grudge against her away. At least then she'd have another Kingston on her side before the rest of the family descended this afternoon.

XANDER RAN A hand across his head, his short hair prickling his palm, and drew a deep breath before turning to his sibling. "What the fuck, man?"

"I could ask you the same question. Are you looking for a repeat of the past?" Dash raised an eyebrow.

"I know what I'm doing. I've thought it through. Not to mention I'm an adult. But forget about me. What's wrong?" Because his happy-go-lucky brother ... wasn't.

Dash liked to show up where Xander was. Even as kids, Xander would wake up and see his sibling sleeping on the floor in his room. But the look on Dash's face now wasn't good, and it had nothing to do with finding Xander almost making Sasha come in the kitchen. And he *would* have had her moaning his name with just the rocking of his hips. Hell, he'd probably have come, too, in his sweats like a fucking teen.

Except they'd been interrupted, and he was still hard and stuck with Dash, who shoved his hands into the front pockets of his jeans. "I think Dominic may quit," he said.

"Hell." Losing their drummer would be a huge blow to the band, who had been together since the beginning. "Want to talk about it?"

Dash shook his head. "I just wanted a breather from the pressure, so I came here. How about you?" He pulled out a chair and sat down, straddling the back. "Exactly what did I walk in on?"

Xander raised an eyebrow. "You need a lesson in sex ed?"

"Fuck you," Dash said, laughing. "You know what I meant."

"I already told you I know what I'm doing." And he wasn't going to discuss his feelings for Sasha with his brother. Hell, he had no desire to think about them himself.

"How about we get the house ready for the family?" Xander slung an arm around his brother's shoulders.

No matter how much he'd rather be continuing what he started with Sasha, he wouldn't throw his brother out when he was obviously in need.

SASHA RETURNED TO her room and pulled herself together. Putting that make-out session out of her mind was impossible, but at least she had something to focus on. If Xander's family was coming over, she needed to make a good impression.

While she thought about what to wear, she called Cassidy, only to find out her friend had decided to visit a relative who lived right outside the city and couldn't make it to the Hamptons today. Which Sasha understood. It was a last-minute invitation.

Standing by the closet, where she'd unpacked a few outfits, she scanned her clothes, including remembering what was still in the suitcase. She didn't want to be too dressed up, like she was looking for attention, nor so casual that it seemed like she didn't care.

She bit down on her lower lip, the same lip Xander had sucked and tugged on a few minutes ago, and shook her head.

Focus. She really wanted his family to approve of her again. Like they had the first time, before she'd blown their lives apart and hurt Xander so badly. They were a tight unit who looked after each other. Sort of like she and her mom ... except her mom had an agenda, to live through her daughter. And Xander's family just poked at one another, joked, and ultimately supported each other. She'd always wanted people like that in her life. At least she'd found Cassidy, who bolstered her in so many ways. And Sasha would like to think she did the same for her friend.

Another glance at the closet and she decided what to wear.

"Romper," she said, pulling the one-piece outfit off the hanger. It was an adorable black and white vintage floral print, shorts not pants, that hung off one shoulder. She bent and picked up a pair of white flip-flops to complete the outfit.

Wanting to give the men time alone, she picked up the script and walked herself through her lines and cues until at least twenty minutes had passed.

Then she walked out of the room and saw them working on the outdoor furniture, moving chairs around a rectangular table. Inside, Sasha made herself useful organizing things in the kitchen, setting up soft drinks at the outdoor bar, and getting the plastic plates and silverware together.

Xander explained they handled clean-up as a family, at least as far as loading things into the kitchen and garbage detail. His housekeeper would come to clean on Monday.

She and Xander would leave the Hamptons tomorrow night. They were heading to Manhattan so they would be close to the set Monday morning. She planned to stay with Cassidy in the new hotel with her security nearby. Which meant tonight was her last chance to be alone with Xander. She wondered if he'd be willing to pick up where they'd left off. She certainly wouldn't mind convincing him.

Midafternoon, a delivery van arrived at the house. Once security checked the driver's and passenger's identification and did a quick search of the inside of the van, a woman and a man wearing collared shirts with a store name on the front unloaded trays of food. Uncooked but premade hamburgers, hot dogs, buns, and a ton of side dishes and desserts were carried inside.

"How many people are coming?" she asked Xander as he directed them through the front door and toward the kitchen. She knew he had four siblings, plus his mom, but the amount of food here could feed an army.

"A lot." He grinned and began reciting names. "Linc and Jordan, she's pregnant, by the way; Chloe and Beck, they're living together and engaged; Beck's two brothers and his parents are coming; there's Dash, the band if they decide to join us, my mom, Aurora, and baby Leah."

"Oh," she said, surprised. She'd expected immediate family only.

"But don't worry. You'll have a fan. My sister Aurora can't wait to meet you. Plus, how can you be uptight when there's a baby around? You have to see Leah. She's got these gorgeous indigo-colored eyes. They're so deep blue." His eyes lit up when he talked about his niece in a way she'd never seen before.

Her eyes widened at the thought of Xander holding a little girl against his broad chest. "You have a soft spot for the baby. That's so sweet."

"I have a soft spot for you," he said, hooking an arm around her waist, pulling her against him, and stealing a kiss that was way too short before the doorbell rang and the first of his family arrived.

XANDER NEEDED PEACE and quiet in his life, but he enjoyed having his family over, too. They were growing, with Linc and Jordan now married, although

Jordan had always joined him at family barbeques, and now Chloe, Beck, and his family. But Xander still didn't consider the extra people intrusive or noisy. Not when he considered them family. Then, he always wanted to hang out with them.

Except for today, when he'd rather be alone with Sasha. Once filming started, they'd be busy, their hours would be crazy, and the eye-fucking she'd been treating him to all day would give way to concentration on work.

After seeing how Dash had treated Sasha the first time he'd laid eyes on her, Xander had made it a point to talk to the rest of his siblings, and thank God everyone had been cordial so far. Even Chloe, his protective sister.

He and Dash grilled the food while they looked out over the pool area where everyone spread out, talking, eating snacks, and sipping their drinks.

"Linc's pretty mellow these days," Dash said.

Xander glanced over to where Jordan was resting, her feet up on a recliner, her belly huge, Linc by her side. "He's got everything he didn't know he wanted."

Hooking up and falling in love with his best friend had been a shock to Linc, as had finding out they were having a baby. But Xander had never seen his oldest brother more relaxed or happy.

Dash studied Linc, too. "I never thought he'd settle down. Not with Dad being such a dick. I thought we all figured we were better off on our own. Except Chloe." She'd chosen a supposedly safe asshole who'd cheated and left her at the altar, leading Beck to rescue her drunk self on her almost wedding day. Beck, who just happened to be Linc's nemesis, but they'd made peace and were working their way toward friendship again.

But Dash wasn't wrong. Thanks to dear old Dad, they were all screwed up when it came to relationships. Their father had been a cheating son of a bitch, hence they'd ended up with a half sister they hadn't known about until after Kenneth Kingston had died. But despite Dash's view of relationships, Xander had always wanted to settle down with the woman he loved.

His gaze drifted to Sasha, who was laughing at something Aurora said while holding Leah up on her shoulder. At the sight of her with the baby in her arms, Xander swallowed hard. Fuck. He couldn't look at her and think about things he wouldn't have. Not with her.

"How do you pick just one woman?" Dash asked, his stare now on Beck and Chloe.

Xander blinked at Dash's stupid statement. "You're a dick," he muttered. "And if you aren't careful, you're going to get yourself in trouble. Aren't you tired of the groupies? Waking up hungover with a strange woman in your bed?"

"No." Dash shrugged, then his shoulders fell. "Maybe. It's complicated and hard to think about when everything else is falling apart."

"Where are the guys?" Xander asked. Dash had gone home after they'd set up the backyard to see what was going on with his band.

"Went home. Dominic is done." He cringed at the statement. "We all need to figure out what the fuck to do now that our drummer is out." Dash ran a hand through his long hair and groaned.

"Cassidy's brother's a drummer," Sasha said, sidling up alongside him. "Sorry. I didn't mean to intrude."

Dash was manning the grill now, so Xander stepped back and slipped an arm around her waist. She looked up at him with wide eyes and a shocked expression. He'd never said they had to hide things, only that whatever they were this time, it had an expiration date.

"Who's Cassidy?" Dash asked, taking the last burger off the grill and shutting off the gas.

"My personal assistant and best friend. Her brother is Axel Forrester. He was with–"

"Caged Chaos. We met at Coachella a couple of years ago. I heard they broke up and he was going solo." Dash cocked his head. "Can you get me his number? Maybe he wants to jam with us. See how we mesh?"

"Sure. I'll talk to Cass later. No problem."

Xander squeezed her side in thanks. She eased herself against him and his cock hardened even more in his shorts, which was saying something considering he'd been in a constant state of arousal since this morning. And again when he'd seen Sasha in that flirty outfit that rippled in the breeze and showed off all her tanned legs and gorgeous skin.

They ate dinner, everyone sitting at the long table he'd bought for just this reason. Chloe and Beck were by his brothers while Xander's mom was near Beck's parents. And Chloe, who, looked out for her brothers, had been friendly toward Sasha, but she was clearly wary, her gaze following Xander's moves any time he touched or talked to her.

The saving grace of the day was Aurora. She'd been so excited to meet Sasha and kept her busy most of the day. Now, over dinner, the baby was sleeping in a Pack 'n Play inside, and Aurora had a monitor on the table. She sat across from Sasha, and Xander had finally settled into a chair beside her, coming in mid-conversation.

"So tell me more about the charity you run," Aurora said. "I read about it in *People Magazine*. They do a monthly feature on people giving back."

He glanced to his right to see Sasha blush. "Once I made it big, I set up a foundation that gives to communities in need. We furnish computers to schools and clothes for kids whose parents can't afford it when their children outgrow what they have."

Aurora nodded. "That's what I read. So maybe you can help me … sometime in the future. I've been trying to decide what to do with … well, my life. I graduated high school but not college, and I don't want to take the time away from Leah to go back to school. I feel like I have so much more life experience than anyone I'd meet there."

Most of the family had grown silent as she spoke, everyone obviously interested in Aurora's plans. Xander hadn't known she'd been thinking about her future. Was she worried? They'd made sure she had a trust fund set up just like all the Kingston kids had from their grandparents.

"I can understand why you'd feel that way," Sasha said, breaking into his thoughts. "I didn't go to college, either. But I was working and trying to make it as an actress."

Aurora used her fork to push salad around her plate. "I know how lucky I am to suddenly have money and options. But I also know what it's like to age out of foster care and have nothing. Literally. I had no place to live, no way to make enough money to pay rent. I'd been working at a diner part-time, and I was lucky they had a back room and the owner let me sleep there. I was able to get work at Dare Nation after that and things turned around for me, but a lot of former foster kids aren't able to recover from being homeless."

And she considered that lucky. Xander shook his head, clenched his jaw, and wanted to punch something for all she'd been through. His father especially but he couldn't change the past. All he could do was be there for his sister now.

"I want to help kids who age out," Aurora said. "That's what I want to do with my money." She fidgeted in her seat and the silence around them was deafening. "I know I'm still young and Leah's a baby, but that's my goal."

Sasha smiled, placing a hand over Aurora's. "I can tell you how we set things up. But it's according to California laws. You'd be doing things in New York, so you'll need to talk to lawyers here to get started. But any questions you have, I'm here. Before you leave, take my cell phone number."

Aurora's eyes filled with tears of gratitude and Xander understood. Coming from nothing, she now had everything. And here was her idol, a famous actress, offering her phone number. Xander was grateful to Sasha for being so open and giving with his sister.

It was going to be so damned hard to keep her at a distance so his heart wouldn't be smashed when she left again – for whatever movie or project awaited her next, in whatever country or part of the world it was set in.

Chapter Six

EVERYONE HAD FINISHED eating and left to do the drive home. Even Dash had taken off early, his mood obviously impacted by his band problems. Chloe and Beck were outside with Xander, and Sasha made herself scarce to start washing dishes. Despite her nerves, she'd had a good time today. She loved how normal Xander's family was despite how much money they possessed and how famous some of them were. Although they'd been told Sasha was staying here, they were obviously surprised, since more than once, she'd caught them watching her. And Xander had given them something to see. They were also obviously shocked by how open and touchy he'd been with her throughout the day.

Join the club, she mused, putting a dish in the dishwasher. She'd spent the afternoon and evening completely caught off guard by the changes in him. Apparently, *sex only* with an end date in sight worked for him. She just hoped she could make it work for her, too, because it was going to hurt when she went home. She knew that much already, before they'd even slept together again.

"Hi," Chloe said, joining her by the sink with some serving plates in her hands. Of all the siblings, Chloe had been the coolest toward her. Not rude, just ... wary.

"Hi. You can put those down. I'll get to them next," Sasha said.

"Oh. Sure." She put them on the counter. "I can take over if you want a break," Xander's sister offered.

Sasha shook her head. "I've got it but thanks." She paused then decided to make conversation. "Congratulations on your engagement."

Chloe smiled, her face lighting up. "Thank you. It's been a whirlwind but so amazing. Umm, are you ready for filming to start?"

"I am."

An awkward silence followed as Sasha loaded the dishwasher and started to wash the plates Chloe had brought in.

Chloe sighed. "Okay, listen, I admit I'm protective of my brother, but watching him today, I see he's happy. And that's all I want. So if I was cold to you today, I'm sorry."

Sasha blinked in surprise. "Thank you." But she was pleased. She'd always liked Chloe Kingston. Sasha didn't want Chloe to assume things about her relationship with Xander. "Your brother and I have an understanding about things this time around."

Chloe narrowed her gaze. "What kind of under-standing?" she asked. "I mean, not that it's any of my business, but you mentioned it so…"

"It's fine. You're right. I brought it up." Sasha shut the faucet. Wiping her hands on paper towels, she turned to Chloe. "It's just that we don't have unreal expectations this time. I live in California, Xander's here, and our lives don't mesh." Every time she said or thought those words, her stomach churned uncom-fortably.

"Sasha, I doubt you know about how I got togeth-er with Beck, but I tried to tell myself I could keep those boundaries. You know, be together while I was living with him and walk away when I moved out." Chloe bit down on her bottom lip. "But that's not what happened, and there was a lot of pain involved before things worked out. All I'm saying is, be careful. You and Xander both."

Sasha's eyes filled with tears, and she turned away despite the fact that it was too late. Chloe had proba-bly noticed. And when she put her hand on Sasha's shoulder, Sasha knew she was right.

"Hey, I was looking all over for you," Beck said, joining them in the kitchen. "Hi, Sasha."

She smiled. "Hi."

"Is everything okay in here?" he asked, glancing

from woman to woman.

"We're all good," Sasha said, meaning it. She appreciated Chloe's attempt to help.

"Great. Because I thought I'd take my fiance home." He strode over and wrapped an arm around her waist, pulling her against him. "Ready?"

"I am." She glanced at Sasha. "Take care, okay? And good luck on the movie."

Sasha smiled. "Thanks."

The couple walked out, leaving Sasha to think. Chloe had made very good points. Sasha and Xander were walking a tightrope and were definitely headed for a fall without the possibility of things working out the way they had for Chloe and Beck. But even knowing that ahead of time, nothing would stop Sasha from making the most of the time she had with Xander now.

THE DAY HAD gone well by Kingston family standards. Everyone seemed to have a good time, the pool got use, there were a couple of arguments that needed someone to referee, and they all ate well. Best of all, everyone seemed to welcome Sasha without giving her shit. All in all, Xander would take it.

He said goodbye to the last of his family – finally – and took Bella out for a walk, waving at Tate as he headed down the driveway. Upon his return, he did a final check of all the doors in the house, closing everything, locking up, and setting the alarm.

He hadn't seen Sasha since she'd said goodbye to his mom and the rest of the family. He stopped by the spotless kitchen, courtesy of Sasha, but all the lights were off. Going in search of her, he headed in the direction of their bedrooms. Her door was partially open, and the sound of the shower came from the bathroom inside. Debating for only half a second, he walked in to join her.

He stripped in her bedroom then opened the bathroom door. Steam greeted him, but as he stepped inside, he saw her. Eyes closed, face tipped up toward the spray, her body even more luscious than he remembered. His cock stood at attention, and he gripped himself in one hand and groaned.

She turned, her eyes opening wide. "Xander."

His dick twitched at the sound of his name on her lips. He pulled open the door and stepped into the large shower, the hot water streaming over them.

Her lips parted in surprise and he raised an eyebrow. If she had a problem with him here, he was out. He wouldn't pressure her–

Before he could finish the thought, she threw herself against him, plastering her naked body against his. He caught her, wrapping his arms around her and lifting her when she jumped so she could wrap her legs around his waist. Holding her again, he finally felt whole.

And fucking horny. It was so much easier to focus on the latter than the emotions rushing through him. Turning, he backed her against the wall, his hips holding her up, his cock hard against her pussy and abdomen. Once he had her pinned, he sealed their lips together, kissing her hard, tasting mint, and wanting more. His tongue swept through the deep recesses of her mouth, devouring her with all that he had to give.

She grasped his head in her hands, just as eager as he was to taste, nip, and consume, but too soon, she broke the kiss. "Let your hair grow so I can grab it and pull."

He grinned, thinking he just might do that. "Lower your legs."

She slid down, her feet touching the floor.

He immediately dropped to his knees. "Now lean against the wall and brace yourself."

Like a good girl, she leaned back and flattened her hands against the tile. He raised her foot and kissed her delicate ankle, sliding his lips up her leg, licking his way over her skin. He paused behind her knee, knowing she liked when he lingered there, kissing that particular erogenous zone before moving up her thigh.

Her hands grabbed for his hair again and she

groaned, instead holding on to his shoulders. Yeah, he was definitely letting the Marine cut grow out. Using his fingers, tongue, and lips, he teased her as he headed north – a very definite destination in mind.

He glanced up and caught her watching him, those striking eyes heavy-lidded and filled with desire. He understood. His cock was thick and heavy, all but begging him to hurry up. But that wasn't his plan. He didn't know how long he had with her, and he intended to slow things down and savor the time they did have.

But as his fingertips drifted upward, gliding over the spot where her thighs met her pussy, she let out a moan, arousal coating her sex, and he doubted his ability to make things last. Clenching his jaw, he slipped a hand over her wetness, and her hips bucked forward.

He knew he had her. Keeping his thumb pressed against her clit, he slid one finger inside, gliding it in and out, gritting his teeth against the tightness he felt there. He added a second finger, and she contracted around him, her hips moving in needy circles, her nails digging into his skin.

"Xander, more, please."

That he could do. He pumped his fingers in and out, curling them inside and pressing against her inner wall. She immediately began to come, her legs shaking, calling out his name. Before he could even use his mouth. Considering the water was going cold, he figured it was for the best.

He kept up the pressure until she settled, her knees nearly collapsing, but he was there. Rising, he held her up. He reached out and turned the shower knob off, pushed open the door, and stepped out before lifting her into his arms. The bed sounded like a damned good idea right now.

SASHA HAD JUST had an amazing orgasm, but that didn't mean she wasn't aware enough to realize Xander was headed for her bed. "Wait! We're soaking wet," she said, her arms around his neck so she wouldn't fall. All the while, they were both stark naked.

"That's why we're going to use your bed. Mine'll be dry for later."

She was about to argue … for the sake of arguing, because honestly, she really didn't mind sleeping in his room. He tossed her onto the mattress, slid down, spread her legs, and all rational thought fled. Especially when he settled himself between her legs and parted her with his fingers.

"Now this is what I've been dying to do all day." He slid his tongue over her sex, and a low moan escaped from her throat.

He licked, sucked, and swirled his tongue over and around her outer lips and her clit, teasing her and tormenting her in the best possible ways. Her hips bucked, but he kept one hand on her lower abdomen, pressing her into the mattress while his tongue worked miracles considering she'd already come in the shower.

As he continued his sensual assault, she writhed on the bed, pleasure building and building until she came apart for a second time.

Xander lifted himself up and wiped his mouth with his hand, a sexy grin on his face. "Ready for more?"

She wouldn't have believed it possible, but her core pulsed with need. "I can't promise I'll be able to come again, but I definitely want to feel you inside me."

His eyes darkened at her statement. "Oh, you'll come." He gripped his large cock in his hand and let out an unexpected groan. "No condoms." He ran his hand over his face, clearly aggravated.

She propped herself up on her elbows and met his gaze. "I haven't been with anyone since you. And I have an IUD." She knew she was taking a risk exposing herself to him, but she did it anyway.

She'd been in love with Xander when things between them had ended and her career had exploded at the same time. Casual sex had not been on her busy radar, despite what the paparazzi and online sites liked to claim about her having relationships with her co-stars.

He was quiet. Too quiet. "Xander?" She looked at him towering over her, his big body still.

"Why?" he finally asked. "Four years is a long time."

She swallowed hard. Her heart had taken a beating after he'd left, but she wasn't going to admit to that right now. "I was too busy working, too jet-lagged, too ... everything, to think about sex."

A smile quirked his lips. "Not even self-provided orgasms?"

She blushed. "I didn't say that." Her handy travel Womanizer did the trick. "Anyway, I'm good to go." But was he?

She didn't want to hear about how many females he'd been with since her. "All I need to know is if you're okay, too," she said.

"I'm good. Yearly physical and all that."

She nodded.

As if he knew the mood had been impacted, he leaned over and pressed his lips to hers, kissing her and immediately getting her going again. His hands drifted lower, shaping her hips, traveling upward, and cupping her breasts. His thumbs played with her nipples, which were suddenly sensitive. He pressed down, plucked and toyed with her until her hips were moving of their own accord.

Sasha knew he could have slid into her now and she'd have taken all of him, but he was stalling. Moving downward until he pulled one nipple into his mouth. Warmth flowed through her along with a stream of arousal as he sucked, then grazed his teeth over the tight bud. She groaned and jerked against him.

"Now, Xander. I need you now."

He pulled his body higher up on the bed and knelt over her, his cock at her entrance. His eyes, the color of midnight, gleamed as he slowly pushed inside her, filling her inch by delicious inch. Yes, he was big and stretched her because he was right. It had been a long time. But as he slid out and in, easing his way, she was so glad she'd waited, because she'd missed this. She'd missed him.

HOLDING BACK WAS tough. Xander's body begged him to *move* but Sasha's earlier admission held him in check. Being inside her again was heaven. Fucking without a condom was up there with the stupid shit he did and would live to regret because nothing could ever come close to this feeling again. Son of a bitch.

But not what he should be focusing on now. "You

okay, sunshine?" He'd always called her that because that's what her smile reminded him of. A ray of sunshine.

She shook her head and he stilled. "I need you to stop trying to be gentle. I'm dying here."

That was all the permission he needed. He pulled out. "Hands and knees," he said, the order coming naturally now that she'd assured him she wouldn't break.

He needed this hard and fast as much as she did. And he definitely didn't want to be face-to-face when he was balls deep inside her without a condom. *End in sight.* No, he didn't want to make this emotional or personal by looking into her eyes.

She immediately got on all fours and he breathed out a sigh of relief. He gripped his dick in his hand and positioned himself behind her. He smoothed a hand over her back and spine, down to her perfectly round ass, gripping it tight.

She moaned and he rubbed his cock at her entrance, finding her so fucking wet for him. Whatever problems they'd had, this had never been it. He notched himself inside her and sucked in a shallow breath.

"Do it," she said, pushing her hips backwards.

He slapped her ass at the same time he thrust deep, and she cried out, her inner walls sucking him in, gripping him tight. "F-u-u-ck. You feel good."

With no need to hold back, he began to move, plunging into her, his balls slapping against her with each thrust. Their pace was frantic yet in sync, nearly perfect as he pounded into her.

He reached around and pinched her nipple, and she cried out, the sound like music ringing in his ears.

"God, Xander. Yes. Right there." She practically sobbed his name.

He held on to her waist, gripping so hard he might bruise her, while giving the quick but deep pace she needed. And then she was coming, his name a chant on her lips that triggered an orgasm so explosive he lost track of time and place. Damned if he didn't feel like he'd blacked out for a minute, and when he came back to himself, he was still inside her, his body still joined with hers.

Their uneven breaths sounded loud in the room. Without warning, she released her arms and legs and collapsed, his dick sliding out of her, and she let out a low laugh.

He fell onto the mattress beside her, facing her. She grinned and he had no doubt he had a smile on his face as well.

"We're wet," she said, her voice husky. "And I don't mean like *that*."

He chuckled and forced himself to roll over and

out of the bed to grab towels from the bathroom. He passed one to her, and while he dried off, she squeezed the water from her hair and patted down the rest of her body, too.

"Want to shower again?" she asked him.

"Depends. Was that it for the night?" Because having had her once, he wasn't nearly finished. He slid his gaze over her naked body and watched as her nipples tightened in reaction. He hoped he could take that as a no.

She raised one delicate shoulder. "I'm up for more. Just one requirement."

"What's that?"

"A dry bed," she said with the sexy smile he adored.

Leaning over, he picked her up once more, this time in a fireman hold. She squealed as one of his hands covered her ass, and he headed to his room, where they could continue what they'd started.

SASHA WOKE UP, and though the bed was unfamiliar, the warm body wrapped around hers wasn't. She closed her eyes and savored the moment with Xander. Last night had been hot and fun. They'd enjoyed each other, which she had to admit brought a new element to their old relationship. He'd been so serious when she'd known him last, and she understood that had been because he'd recently come home from Afghanistan and was still adjusting when he'd found success in his career.

The pressure on both of them in Los Angeles had been intense and their time together was passionate. She liked this newer lighter side of him she'd seen with his family and again last night. Meanwhile, her body ached, reminding her of how many orgasms she'd had and how late they'd finally fallen asleep.

Pushing at the back of her mind was the fact that tomorrow she returned to work, to a hotel, to the life that Xander wanted no part of. Ironic given his backstage presence on set, but she understood him well and knew what he needed to be at peace. Hollywood, travel, and red carpets weren't it. She did not want to think about the future, not when there was still an entire day left before things between them had to change.

And she knew exactly how to start that day off right. Despite knowing Xander was a light sleeper, she pulled the covers down their bodies and slipped beneath his arm. He woke immediately, but she patted his chest and eased downward, making her intentions clear when she wrapped her hand around an erection that was already semi-hard.

She licked the head and he groaned, his hips lifting

off the bed, and she continued, sucking him deep into her mouth.

"Fuck." He wound his hand in her hair, and as she began to glide her lips up and down his shaft, he tugged on the long strands in time to the rhythm she set. The pull on her scalp was as arousing as his slap last night, and her sex pulsed and grew damp.

She had one hand around the base of his cock as she sucked him to the back of her throat, doing her best not to choke. He let out a groan that had her entire body throbbing with need. Using her free hand, she slipped her fingers over her clit and began to rub in uneven, jerky circles.

She wasn't sure how she managed to keep going on Xander and bring herself pleasure at the same time, but she did her best. She pulled him deep into her throat and swallowed around him. With a deep groan, he yanked harder on her hair, and she let out her own long moan, pressing harder on her clit.

"No." He bolted upright, shocking her, and she released him from her mouth. "If anyone's going to make you come, it's me."

Floored he'd been able to think about her when he was obviously so close, she merely blinked at him in surprise.

He reached down and pulled her back to the top of the bed and flipped her over. Next thing she knew, he thrust deep. That's all it took. One thrust and he hit the right spot that had her climaxing immediately, waves of bliss crashing over her. He continued to pump his hips, his cock filling her as she continued to come.

"Xander, so good. Yes, more. Harder."

He listened. He plunged in and out, harder, faster, and she never thought the exquisite sensations would end. She was barely aware when he yelled out her name as his own climax crashed over him.

AWHILE LATER, XANDER had let Bella out back and they'd eaten breakfast while the dog played outside. Then they'd taken a shower, where they'd each managed to behave in order to clean up, and crawled back into bed.

Xander sat, leaning against the headboard, and pulled Sasha tight against him. "We need to talk about this week."

She shook her head and buried it against his chest.

He chuckled and silently agreed. He wished they could stay holed up in his house without anyone disturbing their … reunion? Was that what he should call it? Brief respite sounded, if not better, then at least smarter.

"I figured we'd go back to the city tonight," he

said.

"I thought so." She sighed. "I'll make sure there's a room available for me at the hotel where Cassidy is staying."

He shook his head. "Nothing's changed since you moved out of the last hotel. You should stay at my apartment. With me. I've got a concierge downstairs, an alarm on the apartment, and your security can stay outside the door, watching the hallway. You can't get safer than that." Not to mention, he wasn't ready for her to leave him yet.

She pushed them apart and climbed out of bed, reaching for one of his tee shirts she'd used to go to the kitchen for a snack last night. It hung to her mid-thighs, and he wanted to keep her wrapped up in him forever, but she was already creating distance.

"Xander, we're playing with fire with this. Us." She gestured back and forth between them. "The longer we stay together, the harder it's going to be when it ends."

"Because we're not going to hurt now?" Because he fucking did.

She wrapped her arms around herself, looking as pained as he felt. "I think I should stay at a hotel and let my security stand in the hall there. I'll never be unprotected." Her eyes were wet with tears.

He'd finally made the decision to let his anger go

and allow himself to fully be with her and enjoy her and she wanted to walk away this soon? Oh, hell no. It didn't look like she wanted to go any more than he thought she should.

"Look—" His thought and sentence were cut off by the ring of his cell phone. He glanced over to see Alpha Security show up on the screen. "I need to take this. It's your security team."

She winced. "I left my phone in my room."

He picked up the cell and took the call. "Hello?"

"Speaker," she mouthed at him, and he put down the phone and hit the button so she could hear both sides of the call. "Sasha's here with me. You can tell us both," he said.

"Hi, Sasha. Dan here. I own Alpha Security."

"Hi, Dan."

"So as I just started to say, our tech guys have been going over the emails, snail mails, and gifts sent to you and stored by your PR people. We sorted through the crap and narrowed down ones similar to the one slipped beneath the hotel room door."

She glanced at Xander and he patted the empty spot on the bed. With a nod, she sat down beside him.

"What did you find?" Xander asked.

"A definite pattern. The way the letters are cut out. The type of fonts used and how they've been pasted on the paper. Very crude in this day and age," Dan, who had a scratchy, deep voice, said. "And he was escalating and angry he wasn't getting a response. Not that the PR people caught on."

Xander glanced at Sasha. The color had drained from her face, and he put a hand over hers. "What are you saying?" he asked Dan.

"That you did the right thing hiring us for twenty-four-seven security. Jared mentioned you'd both be at your Manhattan apartment starting tonight."

Sasha's gaze flew to Xander's and her eyes narrowed. He shot her his most charming grin and shrugged. So what if he'd already planned for her to come with him? He hadn't been about to lose their argument and jeopardize her safety.

"Smarter than staying at a crowded hotel," Dan went on. "Makes it easier for the guys to keep an eye on you. We already moved your personal assistant again. To a smaller hotel with fewer rooms per floor. Just as a precaution."

"Thank you," Sasha said in a shaky voice.

"You're welcome. Xander, someone will be by tomorrow to go over your security and I'll get you an estimate. Can you arrange for someone to let him in?" Dan asked.

"Yes." He and Dash had a service that checked on the house in their absence. He'd just shoot off a text to them tonight.

"Anything else?"

Xander looked at Sasha and she shook her head.

"Nothing here," Xander said.

"Okay, I'll be in touch." Dan disconnected the call.

Bracing himself, Xander turned to face her. "Okay, let me have it."

Her shoulders fell and she shook her head. "I can't. You were right. But you still should have discussed it with me before now."

He groaned. "Yeah, I probably should have, but what would you have said?"

"That the hotel was safe with my security, and we shouldn't let ourselves get used to this," she muttered.

Reaching out, he tugged on a long strand of her hair. "Your leaving is going to suck and hurt no matter when it happens," he said in a gruff voice. "Wouldn't you rather savor the time we do have?"

Sad eyes met his. "Yes," she said on a whisper.

"Me, too. But as for the rest of it, it's your life and you need to feel in control in any way you can. So if you're feeling like I'm taking over, let me know."

Her lips twitched, then she spoke. "So you can do what you want anyway?"

Deciding they'd had enough serious talk for the day, he tackled her and came down on top of her sweet body. And conversation was over for a good, long while.

AFTER A LAZY day by the pool, Sasha and Xander packed up, readied Bella, and drove to the city, Jared right behind them. Xander parked in the garage beside his apartment. Only visitors with a phone app could get into the building from the parking structure entrance, which seemed to satisfy both men.

They stopped by the concierge to explain the situation with Sasha staying over and her need for security, both at the front desk and a bodyguard in the hall outside his apartment. Everyone, including his family, needed to be approved with a video call to Xander or Sasha before they would be allowed past the desk.

That settled, they headed up to his apartment and Jared took his position in the hall. Tate would be over at midnight to switch places as they'd done throughout the weekend. Before unlocking his door, Xander had gone as far as asking Jared if they needed to place another man outside the front entrance, but Sasha had balked. She was covered as well as she could be. She didn't want more manpower and resources spent unnecessarily.

Sasha was exhausted and sick of looking over her shoulder. And her ordeal had just started. While in the Hamptons, she'd been able to put the stalker situation out of her mind because she'd felt safe. Xander's house was so far from the city there was no way this crazy human who was obsessed with her could find her. Not to mention, Xander's house was alarmed and her bodyguard patrolled out front. She'd spent the weekend first with Xander's family and later in his bed, her mind on nothing but pure enjoyment.

Apart from the discussion about where she would stay in the city, that is. She'd been trying to protect her heart by pushing for an earlier separation from Xander, but he was right. Was it really going to hurt any less now versus a week or two from now? She was already attached.

She sighed and refocused on her script. Xander was in his office, catching up on emails and working for a little while. She'd made herself a cup of tea and settled into his bed, her dialogue on her lap.

She couldn't deny how normal it felt living with him again. How good. Back in LA, a big, empty house awaited her. True, Cassidy lived there, too, but that didn't negate the fact that, too often, she felt alone. On the road or at home, it didn't matter. There was a hole inside her she'd always thought being a successful actress would fulfill. That's what her mother had promised her. After all, marriage and a child hadn't given Annika the happiness she'd been after. Only the career she'd lost could have done that. But if that was true, why did she only feel that sense of peace wherever Xander was?

Chapter Seven

S ASHA LEFT EARLIER than Xander because she needed to be at hair and makeup by five a.m. After a weekend together, he knew in his gut the start of real life would change everything. Sexually, they weren't just compatible, he'd never experienced anything like being with her. And he'd been pretty active when he was younger, not into relationships, and just set on enjoying himself. While in the Marines, he'd also had no shortage of women who wanted to fuck a guy in uniform, and he'd taken full advantage.

On his return home, he'd been more focused on healing than sex. Until he'd met Sasha. And afterward? He'd bought his home out east, holed up, and hadn't given women much thought. Okay, that wasn't true per se. He'd thought about Sasha plenty, and his hand had gotten a shit ton of use. But the couple of times he'd hit a bar, he'd been unable to pull the trigger and take someone home. No interest. Once again, until Sasha.

Xander walked Bella down the street, anxious despite the fact that Sasha had been with security when she'd said goodbye. Now that they were in Manhattan and filming had started, there was no doubt, whoever this stalker was, he'd be close by.

After bringing Bella back upstairs, he showered, dressed, and headed to the set location downtown, which was a mansion they'd rented to film a party scene. He arrived on the closed set, gave his identification to the security guard, who checked to make sure his name was on the list, and let him past the barricades. He walked up the outside steps and into the house with a marble entryway.

He immediately saw Isaac Reynolds, the director on all the Steele movies, and walked over. "Hey."

"Xander, how are you?" The older man with a big head of salt-and-pepper curly hair slapped him on the shoulder.

"Doing good. Ready to see this book on the big screen."

"Just waiting for our leading lady." He glanced at his watch. "Almost time," Isaac said. "Do you have any idea how fortunate we are to have gotten Sasha at the last minute? This is going to help set up the franchise for a long, solid run."

He nodded. "I'm aware. Where is she getting ready?" Xander asked.

"Hair and makeup is finished. She's waiting in one of the upstairs bedrooms."

"Isaac! Need you over here!" someone called.

Isaac pivoted and went to see what was happening, so Xander headed to the circular staircase and walked up. He caught sight of Jared outside the farthest bedroom and found his target.

"Hey," Xander said, joining him.

Jared tipped his head. "All's quiet," he said as if Xander had asked him a question.

"Good. I'm going to check on Sasha." Before he could take another step to the bedroom, a man with an iPad and headset stopped him.

"No one's allowed back here," he said, eyeing Xander up and down with disdain.

Xander narrowed his gaze. "I'm approved. I'm one of the writers."

"Then I need to see some ID." He puffed up his chest but couldn't come near Xander's size or bulk.

What was with this guy? "I checked in when I got here." Xander wasn't showing his ID to some production assistant with a large ego.

"Curtis, what are you doing back here? You're wanted on set," Marcie Raydor, an assistant producer, snapped.

The guy shot Xander another glare and walked away.

Xander turned to Jared, intending to tell him to look into him. And everyone on set.

"On it," Jared said, pulling out his phone.

Relaxing, Xander stepped up and knocked on the bedroom door. The door opened and Sasha stood before him in full makeup and a gown, and he sucked in a shallow breath. Though he knew the scene they were starting with involved looking for information while a party was going on, he'd forgotten that meant Sasha would be dressed like a queen.

The purpose had been to draw attention to Amanda, Sasha's character, and away from Steele as he searched the house. Right now Xander couldn't think about the story. He couldn't focus beyond the sheer perfection standing in front of him.

She wore a red silk dress that exposed more skin than it covered. Her hair was pulled up in an intricate design, revealing her slender neck, and her cleavage was exposed enough to tempt any man.

He let out a groan and stepped forward, but she put out a hand, bracing it against his chest. "Don't even think about it," she warned him in a teasing voice. "The dress is set and my makeup is on. Nobody will be happy if you kiss it off."

"Except me," he said in a gruff voice.

Her eyes dilated, making him feel better and less … rejected, which was ridiculous. He understood how things worked on set. "I need to go downstairs. Will you be watching?"

He nodded. "You've got this. Go get 'em, sunshine."

She smiled and he escorted her downstairs, stepping aside as she strode into the spotlight. He noted that Jared was downstairs as well, not calling attention to himself but there if she needed him.

For anyone who thought shooting a movie was exciting, they were wrong. Normally it was dead-ass boring. The same scene, shot over and over, and just when they got everything they needed from one angle, they started again with the camera from a wholly different perspective. Hours passed until they took a legitimate long break and Sasha disappeared with her makeup artist for a touch-up.

When the director finally called cut, Xander turned and realized Sasha's agent stood beside him. "Rebecca," he said, recognizing the curt sound in his voice. Fact was, he'd never liked her.

"Xander. Like what you see?" She tipped her head toward the set.

"I do." He'd been damned impressed. Despite the hurt during Sasha's rise to stardom, he'd watched her earlier films. But to view her acting now, with her increased maturity and wisdom, was a thing of beauty.

"She's going far. As long as you don't try and pin her down again," Rebecca said.

And there was the agent he despised. "The only

one who controls Sasha's life is Sasha."

Rebecca pulled her phone from her purse and glanced at her screen before meeting Xander's gaze. "The parts I will be able to offer her will outshine living out of the spotlight and behind the scenes with you." She patted his arm. "Just giving you a friendly warning," she said and walked away, already making a call.

Bitch.

But as much as he despised the woman, she did have a point. Sasha deserved her career and however far she wanted to go. He couldn't and wouldn't stand in her way.

AFTER A LONG day on set, Sasha was exhausted. All she wanted to do was change out of her wardrobe, go home to Xander's, eat something, and crawl into bed. With him. She needed the warmth and security of his big body wrapped around hers, and she wasn't embarrassed to admit it. She'd been glad he was on set, and during her breaks, she always sought him out.

She stepped off to the side and slid out of her heels, holding them in one hand.

"You were brilliant today." Cassidy approached, her eyes beaming.

"Thank you. It's a fun movie. Fast-paced, easy dialogue. We'll have some action sequences. I like it." She glanced around and saw people wrapping up for the day. "Where's Xander?" she asked.

Cassidy laughed. "Somewhere close by, I'm sure."

Sasha rolled her eyes. "It's his book. Of course he's around."

"More like he's watching *you*." Her friend held her iPad to her chest, her gaze growing more serious. "Are you okay? Between this so-called *temporary* romance, a new movie, and a stalker, you have your hands full."

Sasha lifted her shoulders. "I'm fine. And the stalker thing is quiet. Knock wood," she said, lightly rapping her knuckles on her friend's head.

"You're nuts. Just be careful." She glanced at her Apple watch. "I have my security waiting to take me back to the hotel. Do you want me to wait around with you until you're ready to go?"

"No, I'm fine." Sasha wanted to find Xander and leave, too. "Go rest. We have another early call time tomorrow."

Cassidy leaned over and pulled her into a hug. "Talk to you later."

And text, and video chat, Sasha mused, watching as her friend headed for the entrance.

She glanced around again in search of Xander. She'd seen him talking to her agent earlier, and he'd been quiet and more withdrawn from her since. She wondered if he just hadn't wanted to show overt affection on set, which she agreed wasn't professional, or if Rebecca had said something to upset him. The woman was arrogant, blunt, and didn't take no for an answer, which was what made her so good at her job. Not so great of a person.

Sasha felt that same eerie prickle over her skin she'd experienced that day in the city, and she spun around to see if she could locate the cause.

There were production people all over, and one man who looked vaguely familiar stared at her from his position near a camera. No sooner had she caught his gaze than he glanced down at his iPad. She narrowed her gaze. It wasn't unusual for people to stare at her, even on set, but she was uncomfortable nonetheless.

She turned away and saw Xander walking in, cell phone to his ear. Relieved, she walked over to him just as he said goodbye and disconnected the call.

"Hi," she murmured.

"Hey." His gaze raked over her, his eyes darkening as they traveled over her body in the dress that she was ready to take off and the heels that were dangling from her fingers. Still, if the outfit elicited this reaction, that was a plus. "Great job today," he said in a gruff voice. "Perfectly cast."

She beamed, pleased with his praise. "Thanks. It

felt good. But I'm so ready to get out of here. I just need to change."

Jared somehow materialized by her side. All day she'd tried to ignore his presence and what needing a bodyguard close by meant, not wanting to consider the reality of someone trying to hurt her. Or worse.

"Ready to go upstairs?" the man asked, breaking into her morbid thoughts.

She glanced at Xander. "Are you coming with me?"

He nodded and they headed upstairs.

With both men beside her, she stopped at her door and automatically reached to open it.

"I've got it," Jared said. He turned the knob and stepped inside.

She followed and ran right into his back because he'd stopped mid-stride. She bounced backwards and Xander's hands settled on her waist, steadying her.

"What's wrong?" she asked, wondering why Jared hadn't just walked completely into the bedroom.

He turned, his features expressionless. "Xander, get her out of here." He all but pushed her out of the room and closed the door.

She felt the blood rush from her head and dizziness assaulted her. "What? Why? My bag and my phone are in there," she said, realizing the comment was foolish in light of something serious going on, but it had slipped out.

Ignoring her, Jared lifted his cell and made a call. "Send security to Sasha Keaton's dressing room and call the police," he said.

"What happened?" Xander asked, his arm now wrapped firmly around her waist.

"Someone broke in and trashed the room." Jared set his jaw. Arms braced across his chest, he blocked her from going inside.

"Here? How? Everyone inside has been checked at the door. Vetted." She shook her head, her body trembling. "What did they do?"

"Your clothes were scattered and cut up, and there's a note on the mirror across from the door. The same type of cutout lettering used in the other notes," Jared said, oblivious to the nausea filling her.

"You need to make sure the police were notified." Xander's tight voice told her all she needed to know about his reaction.

Before Jared could reply, two uniformed security guards ran up the stairs and joined them outside the room. "The police are on their way," one of them said.

"Good," Xander muttered. "Come on. Let's go somewhere quiet and let everyone do their jobs," he said into her ear, his hands now settled on her forearms.

Jared nodded. "Stay put. They'll want to question

you both."

"We'll be in the empty bedroom at the end of the hall," Xander said.

He started to turn her but she dug in her heels. Or rather her bare feet. "What did the note say?"

Jared glanced over her head to Xander, and Sasha drew back her shoulders. "You're *my* security. This stalker is after me. Now tell me."

Jared nodded in understanding. "The note said, *He can't have you. MINE,*" he said, emphasizing the last word.

She blinked as the words penetrated. "Wait. How does this person know about you?" She spun to Xander. "About us? And how? Has he been following us? Is he here watching?" she asked, panic spiraling.

All day today, she'd felt safe on the closed set and yet somehow … she wasn't.

Time ticked by slowly. Sasha sat on the edge of the bed in the large room, staring at the closed door as they waited for word from someone about the destruction in her assigned room. They didn't talk because there was nothing to say until they knew more.

Finally, Jared knocked and Xander let him in. "Okay, so the police need to talk to you so you can file a formal report. And then we can go home. Right now we don't know anything, but we're running checks on everyone who signed in today."

Xander's jaw clenched and all Sasha could do was nod.

"Are you kidding me?" Cassidy's loud voice sounded from outside the door. "You're questioning me?"

Sasha jumped up from the mattress and strode past Xander and Jared, yanking the door open. A cop tapping notes on his phone stood with Cassidy next to him.

He glanced up. "Ma'am, I just need to know where you were from the time Ms. Keaton went down to film."

"This is ridiculous. Sasha, tell them." Cassidy folded her arms across her chest, glaring at the officer.

Sasha was offended for her friend and assistant. "She was on set all day. I suggest you go looking for the person responsible and stop wasting your time with my people." Reaching out, she pulled Cass inside the room with her.

Shooting her a look, Jared walked out to talk to the officer, leaving the door cracked open behind him.

"I'm sorry." Sasha pulled her friend in for a hug, meeting Xander's gaze over her shoulder. She could hear his thoughts. *They're just doing their job.* She didn't care. She trusted Cassidy.

For the next hour, the police questioned Sasha until they were satisfied they'd gotten all the information they needed.

Xander expelled a harsh breath. "Okay, ladies, it's been a long day," he said to Cassidy and Sasha. "Let's get out of here. Cassidy, do you want us to take you back to the hotel?" he offered.

She shook her head. "I'll go with my security but thanks for the offer." She started for the door and turned. "Xander, I didn't forget about talking to Axel. He's interested in a conversation with your brother. I'll send you his number and Dash can get in touch."

Xander glanced at Sasha, surprised. "You remembered."

"Of course I did. It's important to you." Their gazes met and held, and the heaviness in her chest that had been present all day eased.

"Okay, you two lovebirds." Cassidy clapped her hands loudly and Sasha jumped. "Time to go, like you said."

Cassidy grinned and they headed out, Jared immediately following after them.

AFTER RETURNING TO Xander's apartment, Xander had walked Bella while Sasha took a shower. They ordered dinner and then Xander showered, too, meeting up with Sasha in the kitchen to eat. All the while, his anger and frustration had continued to rise and was near the boiling point. That someone had gotten into Sasha's room in the on-set mansion meant the person stalking her was on the crew. Or had a connection with someone there who'd let him or her inside. His gut churned with mixed emotions from the entire day.

They'd moved into the bedroom, and Sasha walked out of his bathroom and stopped, seeing him standing by the dresser, where he'd just put down his phone.

"Hey, are you okay?" she asked. "You were quiet at dinner."

"After what happened today, I should be asking you that." He studied her, finding it hard to read her expression.

"I'm more in shock that someone who works with me is behind the notes, but I know now I'll have a guard outside my dressing room or trailer at all times. I feel better about that. And I know Jared and the police are working on figuring out the identity of the stalker." She ran her hands up and down her arms. "As far as that goes, I'm okay." She hesitated, then said, "But you aren't."

"I'm fine. Why do you ask?" He was stalling for time.

Her agent's reminder that he was a hindrance to her career had caused him to distance himself during the day. He hadn't responded much when she'd caught up with him between takes, and he'd tried to take a step back. For both their sakes. Then her dressing room had been trashed, which only served to pull him back to needing to protect her. How did he explain that?

She folded her arms across her chest. Her damp hair hung in waves around her face, and her long, tanned legs peeked out from beneath the tee shirt.

Her vulnerability touched the part of him that couldn't keep his distance, and he held out one arm. "Come here," he said, needing to feel her body against his.

She immediately walked into his embrace, and he wrapped his arms around her, holding her tight.

"What is it?" she asked. "It's not just the stalker, because I sensed something wrong earlier today, between takes."

He groaned and led her to the bed, where he sat down and pushed himself against the pillows. Without hesitation, she curled into his side. She trusted him again, and he wished he could let go completely and do the same. But his reasons not to were valid.

"You're talented, Sasha. You already have your pick of roles. And this series is a moneymaker." He knew that from prior films. "When it's over, you'll have opportunities most actresses only dream of. And

I won't stand in your way," he said, forcing out the words.

She placed her hand on his chest and lifted her head. "Rebecca said something today, didn't she? I saw her talking to you, and I knew she was going to try and damage us."

He clasped her delicate wrist in his hand and rubbed his thumb over her pulse point. "Just because I don't like her doesn't make her wrong."

She lifted her head and maneuvered so she sat up and could look into his eyes. "I know we've only been together again for a few days but you feel it, don't you? We're more than just two people sharing a bed."

Her bottom lip trembled as she spoke, and he needed to choose his words carefully. "Even if we are," he began, because admitting to deeper feelings would make it so much more difficult for them both, "what's changed that could make us work?"

She blinked over glassy eyes. "I've grown up, for one thing. I wouldn't let my agent or my mother push me into awkward red carpet walks and fake relationships and things that could damage us."

He nodded, knowing she meant that. He saw the difference in her, the newly found confidence and strength. But that didn't change the bigger issues. "Relationships are hard. They take work. Commitment. Two people in the same place more than they're apart," he said at last.

She sighed. "I don't know how to answer that right now," she said softly, her sad expression tearing at his heart.

"I know." He wanted her to have the world, and he'd give it to her if he could.

Maybe another man could follow her from shoot to shoot, city to city, continent to continent while she filmed but he … couldn't. After his tour overseas, his injury, his time away from his family, he needed a life with peace and quiet. Not one with paparazzi flashing lights in his face or fidelity questions posted in the tabloids.

Which brought up another subject entirely.

He hadn't told her about his father, always keeping that information close, but maybe it was time. "Did I ever tell you why I enlisted?"

She resettled herself cross-legged beside him. "No."

"To get away from Kenneth Kingston," he admitted.

"Your father."

He inclined his head in agreement. "He passed away last year." And Xander felt guilty he wasn't as broken up about it as he thought he should be. Then again, he hadn't really known the man except for his expectations, which Xander and Dash had never met.

Sasha's eyes grew damp, and she reached for his hand, wrapping her smaller one around his. "I'm so sorry."

He shrugged. "I'm not sure I deserve your condolences. He considered me a disappointment, and he wasn't much of a father anyway. I became a Marine because I refused to follow in his footsteps the way Linc had. I needed to be my own man. And I refused to ever become the cheater and spineless bastard he'd been."

She cocked her head to one side, curiosity in her pretty blue eyes.

When it came to his father, the irony was that, at the time Xander had enlisted, they hadn't known the worst of Kenneth's actions. "My father cheated on my mother," he told Sasha. "Not just once but over and over again."

She let out a surprised gasp. "I never knew. I realize I never met him but you always said he was working."

"Because I didn't like talking about him. I still don't." He cleared his throat and ran a hand over his short beard, thinking about the man who'd been emotionally distant and often absent, and his mother who'd ... accepted.

"Mom turned a blind eye. And after Dad died, Linc found a checking account, which eventually led to discovering we had a sister," he said, recalling the day Linc had told him.

Sasha sighed. "I wondered what Aurora's story was. I didn't want to intrude on personal family history by asking."

"It's okay. It feels good to get it out now." Which surprised him. "Both my father and her mother essentially let her grow up in foster care. *He* didn't want to admit to the affair by acknowledging her, and *she* didn't want to raise a child. She'd damn well cashed the paychecks meant for her care, though," he said bitterly.

"That's awful." Sasha's soft gaze met his again. "I guess that explains why it was so easy for you to believe the worst of me—that I'd been cheating on you with my co-star."

He sat up, eased her onto the bed, and straddled her hips, his hands on either side of her head. Shifting, he settled his hips into the cradle of her thighs. She let out a moan and his cock hardened between them.

He forced himself to focus. "Probably. But like you, I've grown up since then. I'd like to think I'd know better now."

Though he couldn't deny that the instinct to believe the worst might always be there. He would just force himself to think more rationally now.

"But none of that changes the distance or the fact

that our needs are drastically different." And he wasn't talking about the desire rushing through his body, hot and thick like molten lava. That need, he knew, was mutual and it was something he could act on. "I'm sick of rehashing things and going around in circles," he said, frustrated. "Can't we just focus on now?" He jerked his hips against her, deliberately running his erection along her sex.

Her cheeks flushed and she wrapped her arms around his waist, grasping his ass in her hands, pulling him closer.

He couldn't control the stalker situation. He couldn't control the future. But he damned well could take advantage of and enjoy the here and now.

SASHA WASN'T ABOUT to fight a battle she lacked a solution to now. She curled her fingers into Xander's ass and rubbed herself against his thick, hard erection.

"Is this what you'd rather be doing?" she asked, her voice husky to her own ears because he felt so good, so hot against her.

He sat up, dislodging her hands as he moved to one side. Then he hooked his thumbs into the waistband of her panties and pulled them down and off her legs, tossing them to the floor. And since he'd only been in boxer briefs himself, he shucked those just as quickly.

Needing to feel his skin against hers, she pulled off her ... or should she say *his* tee shirt and added it to the pile. His hungry gaze devoured her bare chest, and before she knew it, he had her back against the pillows, his mouth on her breast.

He sucked her nipple into his mouth and the pull went straight to her clit. She arched her hips in a silent plea. With a groan, he slid his hand down her abdomen and patted her sex, which only served to heighten her arousal. The damn man was teasing her and she couldn't take it. Not when he was plumping her breast in his other hand, his teeth scraping over her nipple, followed by long swipes of his tongue. Her hips moved in circles, need consuming her. Just from this.

And when his hand actually cupped her sex, she stilled, waiting. Hoping. Finally, he slid one finger back and forth over her lips and pushed a long finger inside, gliding in and out, slick and sure.

"Not enough," she said, panting, arching, trying to suck his finger in deeper.

"Like this?" He pushed that finger back in and brushed the sensitive spot inside her that had her seeing stars.

She whimpered. "Still not enough."

"Fuck." He swung one leg over her and positioning himself between her thighs and, without warning, thrust in deep.

"Yes," she said on a hiss, feeling his thickness everywhere.

He began to move, pumping his hips, taking her hard, and she loved it. Needed it. Because it was Xander and together they were magic. She wrapped her legs around his waist and raised her hips, welcoming every thrust.

She tried to watch him. His jaw was tight, his dark eyes gleaming as they came together over and over. Once again he found that spot, and she climbed higher, so close to coming. Garbled sounds left her throat, noises and words she didn't recognize escaping.

"That's it, sunshine. Come and I'll follow you right over." She caught a glimpse of his handsome face, and then the wave came and she shut her eyes, the force of her orgasm sweeping her out of reality and into some alternate place where all she could do was feel.

As the waves began to recede, she opened her eyes. Xander's hips thrust once, twice, and he let out a loud groan as he found his release. To her shock, ripples of another, smaller orgasm rolled over her, leaving her utterly spent.

Xander collapsed on top of her and she didn't care that she couldn't breathe. Apparently he did, because he rolled, taking her with him. She ended up on top, his cock still semi-inside her.

As his hand tangled in her hair, she thought about their earlier talk. She considered her life and wondered what she really wanted. Was the dissatisfaction she'd felt with her career upon coming to New York tied to acting? Did she want to take it easy? Or walk away completely?

One day into filming and she was enjoying her role. But she didn't like needing a bodyguard around all the time or men thinking she belonged to them threatening her. Then there was the invasion of privacy any time someone recognized her. At times it was fun but mostly it left her feeling empty after. Which was odd, wasn't it?

The only thing that felt good and real right now was the man beneath her.

Everything was mixed up and tangled inside her mind. She sighed. Breathing in his heady masculine scent, she wished this moment could last forever. That they could last.

Knowing it couldn't, something he'd made very clear, she rested her head on his shoulder and hid the tears that threatened to leak from her eyes.

Chapter Eight

ALMOST A FULL week of filming had passed with no stalker incidents. Tomorrow, Friday, was the last day at the mansion. They'd pick up next week in a studio in Queens. Security was tight, and a bodyguard stood in front of Sasha's dressing room door at all times. Though Alpha Security had run background checks on anyone with access to the set and who'd signed in on Monday, no red flags turned up. A handful of people had worked on sets with Sasha before, and Alpha Security was focusing on those individuals because they'd obviously met or seen her in the past. Clearly her stalker had issues, and someone mentally ill could interpret any innocent smile or look the wrong way and assume Sasha was meant to be with him.

Xander had come from a quick meeting with Isaac, discussing the actor playing Steele and his reactions on screen. The director was going to talk to Adrian Hoffman about his over-the-top emotions on screen. Sasha and Adrian, a.k.a. Amanda and Steele, were doing a slow dance toward a new relationship. Steele wasn't certain he could trust the blond woman who'd shown up seemingly out of nowhere to work with him, but he needed to kiss her as a distraction.

Since they filmed out of sequence, the first kiss was up next. Hands clenched, Xander returned to set and saw Sasha and her co-star huddled together in the corner.

He wouldn't lie and say it was easy seeing her with another man, even for her job. But when the filming began, Xander distanced himself emotionally, and the only people he saw were the characters he'd written and an explosively hot kiss that would thrill ... and piss off movie-goers who had been attached to Steele's wife.

And though he'd like to say the experience showed him he could handle her life better now, all it served to do was prove to him how gifted she was and reaffirmed what he'd told her the night they'd talked. She was going places and he wouldn't hold her back.

Hours later, they were in her dressing room at the end of the day when her cell rang. She eyed it, a frustrated look on her face. She hit a button and didn't accept the call.

"What's wrong?" he asked.

"My mother and I'm really not in the mood to talk to her. Maybe later after I've had something to eat, a hot shower, and I've relaxed." She picked up her bag with all her things.

"Here. Give that to me." He took the tote from her. "Ready?"

Before she could reply, her cell rang again. She glanced at the screen and groaned. Tapping on the screen, she put the phone to her ear. "Mom?"

"Hi, baby girl!"

Xander was standing so close he could hear her mother's voice.

"I'm just leaving the set. Can I get back to you later?" Sasha asked.

"Guess where I am?" her mother asked. "At JFK Airport in New York! Surprise!"

Xander met Sasha's stunned gaze. "Why?" she asked.

"Because I miss you. And I wanted to come see you on set. I'm just so proud of you."

Sasha winced. "Umm, I'm happy you're here but I'm really busy. I don't have a lot of time for visiting."

"Don't worry. That's what evenings are for. You can move Cassidy to her own room, and I can take the one connected to your suite."

Sasha shook her head and sighed. "Mom, there's a lot going on here that you don't know about, and I'm not staying in a hotel."

"Why not?" Her mother's voice rose even louder.

"I'll explain it all when I see you in person. In the

meantime, I'll take care of getting you a room and text you in a few minutes where you should go. Call me again when you get settled in." Sasha quickly disconnected the call and looked up at him, her expression tight.

"Are you okay?"

"No," she said, her exhaustion evident by the drop of her shoulders. "Give me a minute to text Cassidy and ask her to get my mom a room. Cassidy already left for the day but she won't mind handling this."

Sasha texted her assistant, then glanced up at him. "I love my mother, I really do. But having her here is the last thing I need. I know Cassidy can work her magic and get her on the same floor she's on. At least the security guard can watch both rooms, but what about when she's out in the city?"

Xander groaned. "She's not a target. Cassidy is with you all the time and, with her long, blond hair, can be mistaken for you from behind. We'll tell Jared what's going on and he'll tell you what he suggests." He stepped closer and wrapped an arm around her, pulling her in close. "Everything will work out."

She nodded. "I hope I can put off seeing Mother until tomorrow, after filming."

"She's not going to be happy when she finds out where you're staying." It was a fact, not a question, and he stated it as such.

"No. But I'm an adult so she doesn't get a vote." She bit her lush bottom lip with her teeth. "Umm … I know we were supposed to go to the Hamptons for the weekend but–"

"Don't worry. We can stay in the city," he assured her. No reason for her to add that to her concerns.

She glanced up, assessing him. "I know how much you look forward to your time away from here though."

He slid a hand through her hair and smiled to reassure her. "I can more than handle being here with you. Don't worry about me. Come on. Let's get you home."

And hopefully they could avoid dealing with her mother for one more day.

SATURDAY MORNING, SASHA woke up in Xander's bed, rolled over, and reached for him only to find his side empty but still warm. He must have gotten up recently.

She sat up, pushing her tangled hair out of her eyes, and glanced around. His glasses were on his nightstand, so she assumed he wasn't in his office working. Maybe he was in the kitchen.

Without warning, Bella came running from the other room, taking a leap onto the bed and curling up by her side.

"Hey, pretty girl," Sasha said, rubbing her fur. "You know your daddy likes you to sleep on your own bed, right?" Because a seventy-pound dog and two adults were a bit much for one bed.

Bella rarely agreed and Sasha liked having her there, too, so Xander had caved. With Bella's head in her lap, Sasha picked up her cell for a quick check before she went looking for Xander. He'd sent a text.

At the gym. Appointment with trainer. Will be there awhile. Enjoy time with your mother.

No doubt he'd escaped to the upstairs gym in the building to avoid Annika's judgmental glare. Sasha didn't blame him.

She'd convinced her mother to enjoy the city and go shopping yesterday, promising her they'd get together on Saturday. Although she'd bought herself time, she needed to shower and get ready to deal with her mom soon.

An hour later, Annika arrived. The doorman called upstairs for permission to let her come up, and Sasha opened the door to let Jared know her mother was arriving, then she waited to greet her.

Her mom stepped off the elevator, looking elegant in a designer dress and heels, as stunning as ever. She saw Sasha and walked toward her, her gaze settling on Jared.

"Who is this lovely man?" she asked, her gaze running over him.

Sasha felt a flush rise to her cheeks. Her mother had no shame. Young men, older men, all were fair game.

"Annika Keaton, this is my security, Jared Wilson. Jared, my mother."

"Ma'am." Jared extended a hand, which her mother eagerly shook.

"Come inside." She gestured for her mother to follow her into the apartment.

Once the door shut and they were alone, her mother pulled her into a hug, and Sasha inhaled her familiar perfumed scent.

"So? Why aren't you at the hotel?" her mother immediately asked, pulling back and looking around.

Bracing herself for an argument, Sasha replied. "This is Xander's apartment, and before you say a word about him, I have a serious stalker situation, and we decided this would be the safest place for me."

Annika stiffened at that, but Bella trotted over to greet her mother, breaking the tension. And Annika, a dog lover, gave the golden lots of love before she rose and said, "Now, tell me everything that's going on."

"Come into the kitchen and let's eat." Sasha had ordered breakfast, to avoid both going out in public and dealing with fans and her stalker. She didn't want to make herself a target and the same went for her mom. If she kept out of sight, Sasha felt safer about the entire situation.

She had everything set up on the counters and took her mother to the large space that even had room for a table and chairs. The apartment was beautiful, and Sasha loved the kitchen with its black cabinets and white quartz countertops.

As if by silent agreement, they made small talk while they ate, her mother telling her stories about friends at home and mentioning a man she'd been seeing. Sasha was grateful he wasn't in his twenties and changed the subject. As far as she was concerned, information about her mother's love life was TMI.

"So tell me more about this stalker," her mother said, finally bringing up the subject.

Knowing she had to fill her mom in, Sasha relayed everything she knew so far. Which amounted to not much.

Annika tapped her long nails against the white quartz table that matched the countertops. "So you're having a problem with a crazed fan and your solution is to stay here? With your ex?" Her mother lifted her coffee cup and took a sip. "I'm not sure I see the wisdom in that choice."

Sasha stiffened. "There's a doorman downstairs and much fewer people coming and going. It's a lot easier to track people entering the building than a hotel. Not to mention, Jared also can focus on his job here."

Her mother sniffed. "I don't suppose you're sleeping in the guest room."

"That is none of your business! Mom, I know you never liked Xander because you see him as a threat to my career, but you were wrong then and you're wrong now." Sasha pushed her plate of eggs aside. She was no longer hungry.

Her mother's expression softened. "You know I'm just looking out for you. You're at the wrong time of life to give away your heart. Not when your career has taken off and everything we worked so hard for is finally coming to fruition. Think back to when you were a little girl. All the commercial tryouts, the rejections ... and now look at you!" Pride shone in her mother's face.

Sasha sighed. "I'm grateful for all you did to help get me here. It's just..." She trailed off and stared at her mother.

Annika was beautiful. Sasha had inherited her blond hair and blue eyes and, at one time, she'd thought her determination to be a star. But even before coming to New York, she'd been tired of the life of an actress, and after being with Xander again, she also questioned the sacrifices she'd already made and the time lost because of them. Still, she *enjoyed* acting, and this film experience was reminding her that her life wasn't all bad. Talk about conflicted.

She blew out a breath and rubbed her hands together in her lap, deciding to focus on her mother's life and not her own. "Maybe *you* were at the wrong time in your career when you met Dad and had me."

Annika's blue eyes opened wide, and Sasha swallowed over the lump in her throat. The idea that she'd kept her mother from pursuing her dreams hurt, but she'd lived with the knowledge her whole life. She'd just never expressed the truth out loud.

"I'm not you, Mom, and I'm not sure what I want for my future. What I do know is that, whatever I decide, it's my choice."

Her mother placed her cup on the table and frowned. "This is Xander's fault. I knew that man would put ideas in your head and try to talk you into staying." She rose from her chair and began to pace the length of the kitchen, her frustration palpable.

Her mother's extreme reaction forced Sasha to feel like she had to justify herself. At twenty-four years old, she was beginning to resent it. "That's not what happened. Xander is the one who has put limits on our relationship. He *wants* me to pursue my career."

And Sasha didn't blame him for the anxiety his tour of duty had saddled him with or the things he needed in order to be happy. She also didn't feel like he was putting his needs ahead of hers. Like her mother, he believed in her talent and didn't want to keep her from further success.

Her mother pursed her lips. Clearly she wasn't buying it. Was it any wonder? She wasn't a Xander fan no matter what she was told.

Sasha decided to keep trying to make her understand because Annika was her mother and she had invested a lot of time and money into Sasha's career. No matter how misguided her reasons.

"I was concerned about my career before I ever saw Xander again. I'm tired," Sasha said, recalling telling Cassidy as much in LA.

Although Sasha had to admit, she wasn't feeling that exhaustion pulling at her here or while working on this movie.

Because here she had more than just acting in her life, a little voice in her head reminded her.

She had Xander's silent support. Cassidy's friendship and the knowledge that her career was in good hands. She also had Xander's family. Aurora had texted earlier, asking if they could get together for lunch to talk about her charity work. Aside from Cassidy, Sasha had had no time for female friends, lunches out, or girls' nights in. Thank God Cassidy traveled with her or she couldn't imagine the loneliness she'd feel.

She met her mother's gaze. "I need you to hear me. I don't know if I want to work this hectic pace anymore. I have a home I'm rarely in, I live out of hotels, and now I have a stalker. Is that the kind of life you wished you'd had instead of being married to Dad and tied down with me?"

Her mother jerked at Sasha's blunt question. "I don't regret having you. I just wish your father had been around so I could have had my career as well." But once Sasha had to be enrolled in school, her mother couldn't travel with him from state to state for gigs, and he'd abandoned them both.

Sasha nodded, trying her best not to let her emotions show. The words were correct but she wasn't sure she trusted them. Her mother's singular focus on her daughter's career above all else told a different story. A sad one.

"Well, it's my life and I'll make the choices I feel are best for me. And if that includes Xander, so be it."

Annika opened her mouth to reply, but as if Sasha had conjured him, she heard the snick of the lock and Xander's footsteps entering the apartment.

He strode into the kitchen dressed in a pair of black running shorts and a royal-blue tank top, stained with sweat. And she was unable to tear her gaze away from the masculine perfection in front of her.

He lifted his shirt and wiped the sweat from his forehead before any fell into his eyes, and Sasha stifled a groan.

"Ladies," he said, his gaze falling on her, a knowing grin lifting his lips.

Her mother turned around. "Xander."

"Annika. How are you?"

Her mother's gaze drilled into him as if she could read his mind from her long stare.

"I'm fine, thank you." She swallowed hard. "Sasha has been filling me in on the stalker situation and why she had to come stay here." She glanced down before drawing a deep breath and meeting his gaze. "I... Thank you for making sure my daughter is safe."

The words were hard for Annika, Sasha knew, and she shot her mother a grateful look.

Xander nodded, jaw tight. "I'd do anything to protect her."

At his words, gratitude and an emotion Sasha absolutely refused to name washed over her. They hadn't put a label on their relationship, nor had they admitted to what each of them felt for the other. Sasha understood his need to protect himself from her given their past, and she couldn't make promises while her career and decisions were so up in the air. She had a film to focus on right now. Choices would have to wait.

"I'm going to shower and make myself presentable. If there's anything either of you needs, let me know." Xander strode off and Sasha watched him go.

Her mother's prolonged sigh broke her focus. "What?" Sasha snapped, tired of the judgment.

Her mother glanced at her, eyes wide. "I don't appreciate your tone, Sasha."

"And I don't want to hear another lecture on choosing my career instead of a man."

Did it have to be an either-or situation? Could she make movies and be a part of Xander's more solitary life? She didn't know. And a big part of her was afraid to find out.

A little while later, she walked her mom out and shut the door behind her, breathing a sigh of relief. Annika was hard to deal with on a good day, and today hadn't exactly been one of those.

She walked into the bedroom to see Xander in a pair of jeans, his top bare, those gorgeous muscles on display. He reached for a tee shirt in a drawer when she spoke.

"Hi."

He turned, shirt in hand. "Hi," he said, his gaze sliding over her, obviously gauging her mood. "That bad?" he asked, reading her correctly.

She gave a little shrug. "As good as it could have been, I guess. My mother's not about to change now."

"When is she going back to LA?" he asked, sounding eager for her to be on her way. Not that she blamed him.

"A week. I think she plans on coming by the set on Monday. Then she's going to visit some friends in Nantucket." She bit her bottom lip. "Is it awful to say I'm relieved she's not staying in the city?"

He let out a laugh. "Not at all. She's not easy."

"I want to say she means well, but ... she just wants to control me so she can say, *Look at my daughter, living the life I could have had if I didn't give up everything to raise her.*" She sighed and rolled her eyes. "I don't want to dwell on it, okay?"

He nodded just as her phone rang from the nightstand where she'd left it, and she walked over to answer. Cassidy's name flashed on the screen. "Hey, Cass."

"Hi! How'd it go with Mom? Anything I can do for you? Get you?"

Sasha laughed. "Oh, just some patience. And a mouthguard so I stop grinding my teeth."

Across the room, Xander chuckled as he finished getting dressed.

"I take it Annika hasn't changed, then."

"No, she has not," she said with a sigh. "What's up there? Anything I need to know?"

"Work is quiet. But guess what? My brother is in town to meet with Dash and the band," Cass said, excitement in her voice.

Sasha knew how close Cassidy and Axel were. "I'm so glad. Will you see him?"

"Xander didn't tell you? We're all getting together tonight. He and Dash planned it earlier. Oops! Incoming call. Gotta run! Talk to you later," she said and disconnected them.

Sasha turned to Xander. "Cassidy said something to me about plans?" she asked with a pleased grin.

He nodded. "We're going to Linc's club tonight at Hudson Yards. It's the safest place we can go since only members and their guests are allowed in. And it's quiet."

"Right up your alley." She walked over and slipped her arms around his waist. "Who's coming?"

He tipped his head. "Let's see. Dash and the band, Cassidy and her brother, Axel, and Linc and Jordan. Aurora wanted to stay home with Leah. And Chloe and Beck had plans."

"So a small crowd of people we like. Sounds perfect."

He pulled her flush against him. "I'm looking forward to a night out with you. You're okay with the plans?"

She nodded. "Sounds like fun." A night with people they enjoyed. A peaceful night that was perfect for Xander and one she was looking forward to so much more than a night on the town with anyone else.

XANDER SAT IN a chair with Sasha close by, talking to a very pregnant Jordan and Cassidy, who, with her long blond hair and her face fully made up, looked remarkably similar to Sasha. No wonder she was worried about her friend's safety with this fucking stalker lurking around.

Linc couldn't take his eyes off his wife, and Xander understood because he was laser focused on Sasha. Relaxed and at ease, she laughed at something Jordan said, the sound light and airy. One he told himself not to get used to, but damned if he didn't want to.

Before he could dwell on that thought, a familiar voice called out. "The guest of honor is here. Let the party begin!"

Rolling his eyes at his brother's antics, Xander stood as Dash entered, the guys in the band following him along with a man he didn't know. "At least we have a private room. Nobody can cheer for you," Xander said, causing Dash and the rest of the family to laugh.

"Axel!" Cassidy rose from her chair and flung herself at her brother, obviously beyond happy to see him.

Sasha glanced at Xander and smiled. He winked at

her in return. She blushed and all he wanted to do was get her home and into bed. Their time together was limited, and as much as he enjoyed being out with her like a real couple, he also wanted to keep her to himself.

Axel, who had the posture and swagger of a musician who knew his worth, stood with Cassidy beside the table where they all sat.

"Introductions," Dash said, clearing his throat. "Everyone, meet our potential new drummer, Axel Forrester. Axel, meet my family."

Linc stood, introducing himself and everyone else at the table by name until he came to Cassidy and nodded at Axel.

"And this is my sister, Cassidy," he said to Dash, whose gaze was lingering on the pretty blonde.

Something Axel noticed if his scowl was any indication. "My sister," he repeated to Dash.

Everyone at the table heard the meaning behind those words. Cassidy was off-limits to Dash. Given his reputation both in the media and in reality, Xander didn't blame Cassidy's brother. At all.

Cassidy treated her sibling to an elbow in his side.

"Oompf. What was that for?" Axel grumbled.

She glanced up at him and scowled but didn't answer his question. Instead, blush on her cheeks, she pulled away from her brother and sat back down in her seat.

"Interesting," Xander heard Sasha whisper to her friend.

"Shut up or you'll get an elbow next," Cassidy muttered.

The rest of the night passed much the same way. Joking, fun, relaxing, and drinking. Xander appreciated his family and knew how fortunate he was to have so many siblings who got along in their own way.

Cassidy rose from her seat. "I'm going to get going. I have a headache," she said.

Before anyone could reply, her brother stood. "I'll walk you downstairs. Your security is waiting, right?"

She nodded. "He's new but seems nice." She turned to Sasha and hugged her good-night, then said goodbye to everyone at the table.

After she'd left, Xander put an arm around Sasha's shoulder. "You okay?"

She nodded. "Getting a little tired but I'm good."

He leaned in and nibbled on her earlobe, ignoring the chatter surrounding them.

Laughing, she turned and whispered in his ear. "Stop that. I can't climb onto your lap here, so cut it out."

His dick hardened at the visual and he was ready to get the hell out of there. "Time to go," he muttered, grasping her hand.

Her eyes gleamed with awareness as she rose to her feet. He texted Jared, who was in the car, and let him know they were on their way out.

As they were saying their goodbyes, a yell sounded from the outer room, and everyone jerked their heads to see what was wrong. Xander's gut churned as he instinctively grabbed Sasha around the waist and held her in place.

"Call 911!" a male voice sounding like Axel shouted.

Sasha began struggling against him. "It's Cass. I know it is. Let me go see what's wrong!"

By now, Linc and Dash had disappeared, heading for the entrance while Xander held on to Sasha, certain this had everything to do with her stalker. He always trusted his instincts, his years in the Marines telling him everything he needed to know.

"Calm down. We'll know something soon," he said, running a hand over her hair.

She stopped fighting him and her muscles relaxed, but the tension vibrating through her didn't.

Finally, Linc walked back inside, his gaze zeroing in on his pregnant wife before he met Xander's gaze.

"What happened?" Sasha asked.

Jordan rushed over to him and he pulled her into his side. "Axel walked Cassidy to the front entrance. Her car and security were outside. She insisted she'd just rush straight to the car and he let her. He said he wasn't as up on the situation as he should have been and assumed her security detail was just standard operating procedure for Sasha and those closest to her." Linc shot Sasha an apologetic look before continuing. "A guy came out of the shadows. He stepped up to Cassidy and apparently shocked her with a stun gun."

Sasha gasped and Xander tightened his grip on her, this time to keep her standing.

"Is she okay?" Sasha asked, her voice bordering on hysterics.

"She's with Dash and Axel and an ambulance is on the way. Axel watched the guy approach, ran out at the same time he zapped her, and yelled. The asshole bolted to his car that was left running. Bastard obviously planned to grab her and go."

Xander clenched his jaw. "Not a well-thought-out plan with her security right there."

"He's not in his right mind," Linc muttered.

"All I know is what happened to her should have happened to me." Her voice cracked. "I need to see her."

Knowing he couldn't keep Sasha from her friend, Xander released his hold. "Come on." He took her hand and led her outside just as the ambulance and a cop car arrived.

Cassidy sat on the sidewalk, Axel kneeling by her side and Dash pacing around them.

"Cass!" Sasha jerked her hand out of his and ran to Cassidy's side. "I'm so sorry," she said, her hand shaking as she reached out to touch her friend's shoulder.

"It's not your fault. He's sick. He tased me and I hit the ground. I think he said *you're not her* ... but I can't be sure. I was a little out of it," she said wryly.

The police and paramedics pushed their way through, taking over, and Jared ran over from where he'd parked the car a few feet away.

"Our guy is escalating," he said.

Xander ran a hand over his face, wanting to get Sasha home, where he knew she'd be safe.

"Where the hell is the bodyguard who's supposed to be on Cassidy?" Jared glanced around, eyes narrowed.

"She said she had someone new today," Sasha said.

He nodded. "So Dan said." He looked over to the car where a man stood off to the side. "Looks like that's him. Don't go anywhere without me from now on."

Xander waited, standing by Sasha as they examined Cassidy, and though she insisted she didn't need the hospital, Axel disagreed.

"I'm okay. I swear," Cassidy said, her arms

wrapped tightly around herself.

To Xander's shock, Dash knelt down, meeting her gaze. "You're going to get checked out and make sure that's true," Xander's brother said through gritted teeth.

"What's with Dash?" Sasha asked, turning her tear-stained face up to face him, and Xander's heart squeezed tight in his chest.

He reached up and swiped a stray tear from her cheek. "I don't know. Seems like he was struck by lightning when he saw Cassidy," Xander said, attempting a laugh, but the entire situation was stressful and not funny.

They'd begun to attract an audience and he wanted her out of the spotlight. Cassidy had agreed to go to the hospital, and Axel hopped into the back of the ambulance along with her and Dash strode up to them, his expression tight.

"What the fuck are the police doing about this asshole?" he asked.

"I heard them say they'd take her statement at the hospital," Sasha said. "And I want to be there."

Dash nodded. "Me, too. Let's go."

"Wait." Xander grabbed his brother's arm. "What's your interest in Cassidy?"

His brother narrowed his gaze. "Why do you care?"

"Because she's Sasha's best friend and I know you." He pointed, hitting his brother's chest with his finger.

"Hey." Dash grabbed his finger. "You're *my* brother. Where's the faith?"

Sasha looked back and forth between them, her impatience showing on her expressive face.

"Did you wake up alone this morning?" Xander asked.

"Well, no, but—"

Xander put a hand on his shoulder. "But that's why. I don't want Cassidy hurt. And you have that determined look on your face. So unless and until you get your head in the game and know what you want, you need to leave her alone."

"And as Cassidy's best friend, I agree. If you hurt her in any way, I'll kill you, Dash." She looked at Xander. "Can we *go* now?"

He watched the wheels turn in his brother's head, and finally Dash came to a conclusion. "Fine. But I'm still checking on her at the hospital."

Xander nodded. Though he'd rather take her home, he respected and understood her need to make certain her friend was okay.

Chapter Nine

BEYOND EXHAUSTED AFTER hours at the hospital, Sasha dragged her body into Xander's apartment. Bella came barreling out to meet them, and Sasha knelt down to give her attention after such a long stretch of her being alone. Then she rose and kicked off her heels, leaving them by the door. Her feet were killing her. The shoes were meant to wear for an hour or two, not to pace a hospital emergency room.

Xander grabbed Bella's leash from a hook by the door. "Back in a few minutes. Lock up until I return."

Since their emotions were raw from Cassidy's attack, she promised she would, no argument or jokes about Jared being right outside.

After they'd left, Sasha leaned against the wall and let out a groan. Thank goodness Cassidy was fine, no damage from the Taser or her fall, for which Sasha was relieved. Still guilt-ridden but relieved because her best friend wouldn't have been in a position to be attacked if the stalker hadn't thought she was Sasha.

She walked to the kitchen and pulled out a bottle of cold water from the refrigerator. She took a long drink before heading to the bedroom, sitting down on the bed and leaning back against the pillows. She closed her eyes for a few minutes and was shocked to realize she'd dozed off, only waking up when Xander returned and she heard the beeps of him setting the alarm.

She pushed herself to a sitting position and met his gaze as he walked into the room. "Hey."

"Hi. Bella was fast and she didn't seem to need a long walk."

She smiled. "She's such a good girl."

He laughed. "For a dog who failed her service test, yes, she is. She's a great companion."

She chuckled, then sobered, remembering the events of tonight. "I'm glad Cassidy and Axel are staying at Dash's place in the city tonight. She shouldn't be alone in a hotel room. But thanks for offering up your spare room." It had been extremely sweet of him.

"I knew you'd want her close." He shrugged as if the gesture was no big deal.

Which was exactly why it was one. He cared about what she wanted. Needed.

"Tired?" he asked.

She nodded. "I fell asleep while you were out." Before she could blink, he'd walked over to the bed and scooped her into his arms.

He walked her straight to the bathroom, lowered her to her feet, and pressed a kiss on her cheek. "Go shower off the feel of the hospital. You'll sleep better if you do." He turned and started toward the door.

"You're not joining me?"

He turned back to face her, his eyes darkening at the prospect, but he shook his head. "Not a good idea if you want to get any sleep," he said in a gruff tone that turned her on anyway.

She couldn't deny the fact that she needed rest, but she grabbed his face and pulled him close, sealing her lips over his. He hooked his arm around her waist and hauled her against him, his tongue spearing past her parted lips, and suddenly she wasn't tired anymore.

She lifted his shirt and pulled it over his head, then braced her hands on his well-cut abs. He met her gaze and grinned. "No sleep?"

"After." She reached for the button on his jeans, pulled down the zipper, and slid her hand in, wrapping her palm around his thick erection.

"Point made." He stripped off his jeans, kicking them aside, and while he added his boxers to the pile, she quickly undressed, too.

She linked her arms around his neck and hopped up, wrapping her legs around his waist. He walked her to the bed and laid her on the mattress, his body coming down over hers. His cock pressed hard and insistent against her belly, and her sex pulsed with desire.

"I need you," she whispered, running her fingernails over his hair and scalp.

He shifted his hips, his cock slid through her wetness, and he let out a groan. "And I need to feel you hot and slick around me so I know you're here and safe."

She met his gaze. "It wasn't me who got hurt," she reminded him.

"But it was meant to be you. And I couldn't take it if something happened to you."

Tears filled her eyes at the sincerity and caring in his tone. "I'm fine," she assured him, grateful to be here with him.

Not wanting to wait, she spread her legs and his hips settled in the cradle of her thighs. A low, guttural sound escaped his throat as he braced his hands above her shoulders, poised himself at her entrance, and easily slid into her.

His gaze remained on hers, those breathtaking eyes holding her captive as he began to glide in and out, her entire body aware of his thickness and length filling her completely, rubbing against her as he eased out only to sink in deep again.

She expected hard and fast. After all, they'd had a long, trying day and night, and she figured he'd want to relieve his frustration with the stalker situation by losing himself in fast and furious sex. Instead, she found herself with a gentle, caring Xander and it scared her.

Scared her because, as he held her stare, her emotions rose to the surface. A rush of warmth and feeling swept over her along with a need for him that ran deep. One she wasn't certain she could escape a second time. She wasn't sure she wanted to.

He began to move faster, his hips pumping against her, his pubic bone hitting her in just the right spot outside while his cock rubbed the perfect area inside her. The waves crested quickly, but they were no less spectacular because they were fast. If anything, the emotions she couldn't fight combined with the perfection of their union.

He wasn't fucking her, sleeping with her, or merely having sex until their time together ended. This was making love, and as she climaxed, her body suspended in a place only Xander could take her, she heard sobs and whimpers, sounds she didn't recognize. Sounds she made.

And then his motions became faster, more frantic and out of control. There was the fast and furious pace she'd expected, but as his climax hit, there was no distance between them. They came together as one perfect whole.

★　　★　　★

SASHA RETURNED TO work on Monday, and though she insisted Cassidy stay home and rest, her friend was on set, iPad in hand. She'd spent the night at Dash's apartment after the attack, her brother by her side, to appease his worry. The next day, she insisted on returning to her hotel room and living her life. Sasha had tried to convince her to move into Xander's spare room, but she lost that battle, too. Her strong friend would do what she thought was best and Sasha admired her for it.

They'd finished filming at the mansion and were now on the main set in a studio, and Sasha had her own trailer. Jared, of course, was standing nearby, and another man was watching her trailer door. She had spent hours on Sunday going over her script and character and had come in early to run lines with Cassidy.

Her co-star, Adrian, was a nice guy with enough of an edge to play Steele, the focused, man-on-a-mission Marine. Sasha felt enough chemistry with him to know their scenes together were electric, a gift that didn't happen with everyone she worked with. And though she sensed Xander's tension during their emotionally and sexually charged scenes, he never brought jealousy between them after the director called cut. Not even after the first kiss scene.

On the other hand, having her mother on set was a challenge. First, Annika had introduced herself to everyone she deemed important, reminding them of the smaller roles she'd had in movies that ... no one knew about. When that effort failed, she began to declare to all who would listen, and even those who didn't, that she was Sasha's mother and had given up so much to get her daughter where she was today. It reached the point where Sasha was grateful when filming started and everyone had to be quiet.

Except while she was working, she caught sight of her mother and her agent with their heads together, talking, laughing, and nodding, clearly in agreement on *something*. And Sasha had a feeling she wouldn't like what they were discussing.

"And that's a wrap for the day. Sasha, we've moved quickly. Two, three more days max for you," Isaac said. "Great job."

She smiled at the director, grateful for the praise. "Thank you," she said and walked toward Cassidy, who waited behind the cameras.

"I'm starving," Sasha said to her friend. "What do you say we get dinner? Just you and me? We can talk." Sasha needed to see for herself that her friend was okay.

"What about Xander?"

Sasha grinned. "He'll understand we need girl

time."

He'd left the set to have lunch with his agent, satisfied Sasha had Jared by her side and Rhodes, the extra security agent, by her trailer door.

Her friend's eyes sparkled as she nodded. "Time together would be great."

"Perfect," Sasha said. "Just let me say goodbye to my mother." She gestured toward where Annika was chatting up a guy who worked on the crew. He looked familiar to Sasha but didn't strike her as being important enough for her mom to waste time on. It wasn't the way Annika operated.

She walked over, and to Sasha's surprise, her mother shot her a look of utter relief. "Sasha, there you are. I was just trying to tell this … chatty man I have a car driving me to Mackinaw City. My friends are meeting me at the ferry when I get to Nantucket."

"And I was just telling your mother that you and I go way back," he said, his gaze raking over Sasha. "I worked with you on a few of your movies, right?" The man, who appeared to be in his early thirties with brown hair and eyes, smiled at her in a way that was too … much.

Sasha narrowed her gaze, trying to remember, but there'd been so many movies and so many faces on set. Still, not wanting to be rude, she played along. "Umm, right. Mom, come on. I'll get you to your car."

She turned away from the man and faced her mother. Before she could speak, Jared walked over, joining them from where he'd been doing his job, always waiting, always there. "Everything okay?"

Sasha nodded. "My mother was talking to that guy—" She turned to point out the man but he was gone.

"He was boring me with stories of his times on set with Sasha. As if he were someone important." Annika waved a hand, obviously dismissing the guy.

She glanced at Jared.

"I saw him but I've seen you both talking to quite a few people on set. What was his name?" Jared's steely gaze swept the area.

"I don't know. He assumed I knew who he was," Sasha said, wrapping her arms around herself.

"Ms. Keaton?" Jared looked to Annika for answers.

Annika shrugged. "How would I know? I forgot it as soon as he told me." She glanced at her watch, obviously worried about making her ferry.

Uneasy, Sasha looked to Jared. "Can we get her to the car service we arranged?"

Jared nodded. "I'll get someone to take her out—"

"Sasha." Xander called to her as he approached from across the room.

"Hey," she said, relieved he was here.

"What's going on?" he asked.

"Jared is going to take Mom to her car. I'll explain while we head to my trailer." Now that Xander was with her, she could let Jared take her mom.

She turned to Annika. "Have fun with your friends. I love you," she said, hugging her mother.

"Me, too." Her mom squeezed her back, speaking softly in her ear. "I know I'm hard on you but I just want great things for you." She smoothed her hand over Sasha's hair. "And Rebecca has big things to talk to you about. All our dreams are coming true."

Sasha winced at that, but she wasn't going to fight with her mother right before she said goodbye. "I know, Mom. Have a safe trip and enjoy your time with friends."

Sasha's mother slid her arm into Jared's, who appeared uncomfortable. He glanced at Sasha. "I'll meet you two at your trailer." He pinned his gaze on Xander. "Don't leave her side," he said, then walked her mother to the exit.

"What was that all about? Did something happen while I was out?" Xander asked.

Knowing he'd lose his mind, she prepared herself, then went into detail about the crew member who had latched on to her mom and claimed he and Sasha went way back.

"And you don't remember him at all?" he asked,

then clenched his jaw tight.

"No. Jared will do a sweep looking for him after he gets my mother off safely." And since she was with Xander and had a guard at her door, she felt protected. "I told Cassidy we could get dinner together and catch up."

"No."

"I—" She cut herself off before she could snap back that he couldn't tell her what to do and drew a deep breath instead. His worry was genuine.

Xander placed a hand on her back. "Cassidy can come to my apartment for dinner. The last thing we need is another incident with you two out in public. Cassidy got lucky on Saturday night. I don't want to tempt fate. Or the stalker," he muttered. "I'll even make myself scarce so you two can be alone to talk."

She smiled. "You can hide out in your office and work. No need to go anywhere."

He let out a relieved breath. "Okay, we're in agreement. Good. Now, I want to get you out of here. Where's Cassidy?"

"Over there," she said, pointing to her standing beside her security guard.

A few minutes later, she and Cassidy were in her trailer, where Sasha washed off her makeup and pulled her hair into a ponytail. She explained the wisdom of ordering in dinner instead of going out and Cassidy agreed.

Then they met up with Xander and their respective security details and headed to Xander's apartment for dinner.

An hour or so later, Xander took Bella for a long walk, while Sasha and Cassidy ordered in a cheap dinner of Chipotle burrito bowls.

"This is so good," Sasha said, taking another spoonful, and Cassidy agreed.

"I needed a chill night like this." She patted her mouth with a napkin and leaned back against her seat with a sigh.

At a glance, to a stranger, Cassidy appeared fine. To Sasha, who knew her well, she took in the light circles under her eyes, and she narrowed her gaze.

"Are you really okay?" Sasha pushed aside the food she hadn't yet finished and focused on her friend.

"I admit I'm still shaken up from the attack." She met Sasha's gaze. "I didn't want you to add worrying about me to everything already on your plate."

"That's ridiculous! You're my best friend. Practically my sister. You matter, Cass. What can I do to help? Do you want to go home to Adam? I already told you that-you can work from home. I don't mind at all." Anything to make Cassidy feel better and safe.

She shook her head. "The asshole broke up with me on Friday. By text."

"After all the years you were together, that's how he ends things?" Sasha was horrified and angry for her friend. "I'm going to kill him."

Cassidy gave her a half smile. "I appreciate that. I was going to tell you when I saw you on Saturday but … things happened."

"How upset are you? On a scale from one to ten?"

"Three? And that's the part I don't understand." She leaned forward, one hand under her chin. "I think with all the travel, we drifted apart and neither one of us did anything to stop it. Maybe we didn't care enough?"

"Oh, I think you cared plenty. It's just that, yes, sometimes people drift. Or they come into each other's lives for a purpose, and when that need is served, you move on." Sasha lifted her shoulders. "I'm just glad you aren't heartbroken."

"I'm not," Cassidy murmured. "I'm glad we never moved in together. Another sign things weren't meant to be."

Sasha knew Axel and Cassidy's parents died in a car accident when they were young. Their grandmother raised them until she passed away when Axel was eighteen. He'd always felt responsible for his sister, and Cassidy had sometimes felt stifled by his overprotective nature and just wanted to live her life.

Sasha wondered now if Adam had been Cassidy's

way out of being under her brother's constant scrutiny. She didn't want to upset her friend by asking.

Besides, there was something else Sasha wanted to know. "How was your night at Dash's place?" She'd never seen Xander's brother so concerned about a woman. Not in his early days of fame when she'd first met him, and Xander had obviously not seen him act that way since.

A blush rose to Cassidy's cheeks. "He was actually sweet. Really worried, you know? He had to sneak around my brother to actually check on me, but I appreciated it."

Oh, no. Sasha knew that look on her friend's face. "You cannot fall for Dash Kingston. He lives and loves his rock-star lifestyle. And Xander has said he doesn't see his brother settling down."

"What? I'm not," she said too quickly, making Sasha question the denial. "I know the lifestyle well from Axel. He's no saint with women, either. Trust me." She picked up her glass and took a drink. "Now why are we so focused on my life? I'd rather talk about what's going on with you and Xander?"

It was Sasha's turn to flush. Just the thought of Xander and his hands on her body could do that to her. "Things have gotten intense." She rose and began to collect the garbage and walk over to the trash can, tossing it in.

"What are you going to do about … everything?"

She lifted her hands, exasperated. "I wish I knew. Rebecca says she has something to discuss when my part of filming is over. She doesn't want to distract me from work on this project." And every time she thought about the future, her stomach twisted into uncomfortable knots.

Cassidy rose and walked over, clasping her hands. "Whatever you do, whatever you decide, I've got your back."

Sasha threw her arms around her friend and hugged her tight. "You're the best, Cass. And I hope you know the feeling is mutual." She released her too tight grasp and stepped back. "Just know you can leave, stay, hole up, do anything you want until this mess blows over. I'm here for you, too."

"Well, I'm staying."

Sasha let out the breath she hadn't been aware of holding. "And I'm so glad."

XANDER TOOK BELLA on an extra-long walk. Not only because he wanted to give the girls time alone but because he needed to destress. He'd been in the city over a week now, and with the added pressure of Sasha's stalker and the end of her filming creeping up on them, he felt a heavy weight sitting on his chest.

He'd have to be blind not to see her agent on set talking with Sasha's mother, no doubt both of them planning her future. Was it a future she wanted? One she'd allow them to talk her into having? Or, as she'd said, was she different now? Ready to take control of her life?

Bella paused to do her thing and he waited patiently. The streets were quiet because it was summer and residents left for the beaches. But a car drove by, honking at another vehicle that cut him off, leading to the opening of windows and yelling back and forth. God, he hated Manhattan and he missed the view of the water.

He cleaned up after Bella and tossed it into the nearest garbage can before continuing their walk. His cell rang and he pulled it from his pocket, answering when he saw it was Aurora calling.

"Hey!" He was happy to hear from her. "How's my adorable niece?"

"Leah is good, thanks! She's been sleeping through the night for a while now, so I've been feeling more human. How are you doing? How's Sasha?"

He grinned. Aurora was a lot of things but subtle wasn't one of them. "We're good ... for now," he admitted, not wanting his starstruck sister to get her hopes up that Sasha would be around and in their lives for much longer. His gut cramped at the thought.

"What does that mean? I saw you two together. You're as perfect a couple as Linc and Jordan or Chloe and Beck."

Arriving at a corner, he waited for the light to turn and crossed the street. "Don't tell me you're a romantic," he teased her in an attempt to distract her from his relationship with Sasha.

She snorted in his ear. "Me? Are you kidding? No. I'm a realist about life."

Xander narrowed his gaze. In the eight or nine months since he'd met Aurora, she'd never mentioned the baby's father. As far as he knew, nobody in the family had asked about him, either. Aurora was more adult in her thinking and more reserved about her feelings than most people her age, no doubt because she'd been in foster care and alone, practically raising herself. She was an exuberant young woman but not forthcoming about her personal situation.

Ah, well. Xander figured they had time to push. Right now she was thriving and learning to accept their family closeness and being a part of it.

"I just want you to be happy and it seems like Sasha does that for you." Aurora's voice pulled him out of his head and back into their conversation.

"She does but she has a career that keeps her traveling, and her home base is in LA." He really didn't want to continue this discussion. "Don't worry about it. I'll figure things out."

"I hope you do. I like her," Aurora murmured. "Meanwhile, while Sasha is in town, I really want to get together and talk to her about her charity."

Xander reached the next block and steered Bella left, planning on circling back to his apartment. He thought about Aurora's question, and despite wanting to agree, he knew he had to nix the possibility for now. Like Sasha, Aurora was blond, and Xander didn't want her to be seen with Sasha or, worse, mistaken for her as Cassidy had been.

He explained the situation to his sister. "When this guy is caught, I'll make sure you get time with Sasha."

"Thanks, Xander. I hope Sasha and Cassidy are okay," Aurora said, more subdued now.

"I'm making certain they will be."

"I know. Nobody will get to her if you're around."

He smiled at her. "Thanks for the vote of confidence."

Her laughter lit up his mood.

They talked until his apartment building came into view. "I'm home. Gotta run. I'll call you again soon."

"Bye!"

Xander disconnected the call, his mind on his promise to his sister, that he'd make sure she saw Sasha after the stalker situation ended. Of course, that assumed she wouldn't be on the first flight back to LA when her filming was finished.

They hadn't had that conversation yet and he didn't want to think about the end … but maybe it was time they were realistic about her plans and what it meant for them.

As he entered the building, nodding to the doorman and walking into the elevator, an idea came to him. One that would stall Sasha's departure and give them a special weekend together, whatever her final plans turned out to be. He just had to figure out when to make the suggestion, then hope she said yes.

Chapter Ten

S ASHA SPENT TWO more days on set and she wrapped her final scene. Relief washed over her as she walked straight into Xander's arms.

"You are amazing." He hugged her tight and she inhaled his masculine scent, the one she found so arousing.

Unable to help herself, she buried her face in his neck and kissed him there before stepping back.

His darkened gaze met hers, and he grasped her hand and pulled her aside, into a darkened area on set between racks of hanging clothing. Once they were alone, he sealed his lips over hers and thrust his tongue into her waiting mouth. His kiss was hot and sensual, his tongue tangling with hers for a good long while until he raised his head and met her gaze.

"Go away with me," he said in a gruff voice.

"What?"

"Before you make any decisions about your future, before you leave New York for good, spend the weekend with me. We can go to my house in East Hampton or go somewhere in the Caribbean. Dash can take Bella and we can leave tonight."

She blinked in surprise, unsure what to say. "I'd love to but I have things to wrap up with my agent, and I hadn't decided what I wanted to do yet about ... anything." Looking up at him, she saw the hurt in his expression before he quickly masked it.

"I understand." He stepped back and she grabbed his arm.

"No, you don't. Just ... give me a day to think and wrap up some things and we'll revisit the trip, okay?"

He inclined his head. "Of course." He turned and headed back to the main area, leaving her to follow him, her heart in her throat.

Goddammit. She hadn't meant to hurt him. The last couple of days between them had been magical. After Cassidy left the apartment on Sunday, Xander had returned from walking Bella, and they'd fallen into bed. And they hadn't gone to sleep, either.

If she'd thought their night after Cassidy's attack had been intense, the last couple of days, she and Xander had been insatiable. And it wasn't just a sexual thirst for one another, either.

They'd talked. Mostly she had. She'd shared deep, meaningful discussions that ripped open old wounds as she'd let him in. He'd already told her about his father and mother and the issues he'd had with them.

And she'd opened up about her dad and the hole

his leaving had left in her life.

"My dad walked out when I was ten," she said. "Old enough to realize what was happening and to blame myself, something my mom managed to reinforce, often."

"I'm sorry. She should never have put so much on your shoulders. She's the only one responsible for her life." Xander curled around her, giving her his strength and himself.

"Sometimes I can push it all aside and then she comes around and tells me what I should want out of my life and reminds me of all she's sacrificed to get me where I am." Sasha leaned into his strong arms and relaxed against him, appreciating his quiet understanding.

"You know, what I said about your mother applies to you, as well. You are responsible for your life. So you need to decide what you want. What will make you happy."

To his credit, he never asked her to give up her career or to choose him over acting. But with her time in New York drawing to a close, she had so many thoughts and questions going through her mind.

What *did* she want? Could she leave the man she knew, without a doubt, that she loved? What choices were smart for her future and not short-sighted because she didn't want to lose him a second time?

One conclusion she'd reached was, even if she continued to act with the schedule she'd been keeping, no relationship could survive. If she cut back, she had hope she and Xander could attempt to make their lives work, but she didn't think either one of them would be truly happy with a long-distance relationship. So it all came back to that elusive question he'd asked her.

What, exactly, did she want for her future?

Xander walked away, his phone in his hand. At a loss as to how to make him understand, she decided to give him some space.

Jared caught her gaze and strode over. "Ready to go to your trailer?"

She nodded. "Thanks." They started walking and Sasha found herself frustrated, not just with life but with this entire need for constant security. "Anything on the stalker?" she asked.

Jared shook his head. "Unfortunately, no. Everyone who has worked with you before has been checked out. No history of violence or mental illness by anyone on the list."

Sasha sighed. "Where is Cass?" she asked, still worried about her friend.

"She went back to her hotel to rest."

Sasha wrapped her arms around herself, upset that Cassidy had been hurt because of *her*. "Despite her being checked out by a doctor, she's having a hard time since the attack."

"Understandable," Jared said. "Being Tasered is painful and frightening." He stopped outside the trailer. "Here we are."

The trailers were located on the outskirts of the set, and since her co-star was still filming at another location, it was quiet here now, no people milling about except for her second security guard.

"Hey, Rhodes. All quiet?" Jared asked.

He nodded. "Nothing to worry about."

"Good. I'm going to check in with the office. I'll be back to walk you to the car when you're ready to leave. Just text me."

She nodded. Rhodes watched the trailer but Jared was her main detail and driver. Tate still took over late at night.

Jared strode away and Sasha walked into her dressing room, closing the door behind her. A metal pitcher of water sat on a high snack table nearby, and she poured herself a glass, then sat down on the soft couch and tried to relax, needing a few minutes to pull herself together. Then she'd wash up, change, and get ready to head back to Xander's. And that wouldn't be enjoyable given his reaction earlier.

But what did he expect? He'd sprung the trip idea on her. Leaving tonight, of all things. She'd just wrapped her role, she had Cassidy to talk to and plan their return to California. Her stomach lurched at the thought of leaving Xander, and she rubbed her hand over her eyes, not caring about smudging the makeup she intended to remove anyway.

God. Why couldn't she just stay in one place and have control over her career and what movies she did and when? Without the pressure of people pushing her to accept more and more roles? To choose between her personal life and her profession?

She sat up straighter as an idea came to her. She absolutely could do what she wanted. What if she formed a production company where she could pick projects she loved? She'd be able to both create and buy content, star in a project, or work behind the scenes. She certainly had the cachet to attract star talent, the ability to obtain start-up funding and take in a partner if she wanted.

Her heart began to beat rapidly in her chest as the concept formed. And because it excited her more than acting in another movie right away, she knew she was on to something. This was a new dream she could make a reality, and she couldn't wait to tell Xander.

Her trailer doorknob turned, the noise catching her attention. Only Xander or Cassidy would get past Jared and be allowed in unannounced, and Cassidy was gone for the day.

"Xander!" She hopped up from the sofa, eager to see him and explain her reaction earlier and make it up to him when she told him about her new idea.

Except the person who walked into the trailer wasn't Xander.

The brown-haired man who had been talking to her mother earlier stepped inside and pulled the door closed behind him. Hands behind his back, he pushed the lock on the doorknob.

The click sounded too loud in her ears. "What are you doing in here?"

"You know you've been waiting for me to get you alone." He had a gleam in his eyes that made her uneasy, and she was already freaked out that this guy was in her trailer.

"Where's my security guard?"

"I'm afraid he had to be taken care of. I couldn't get close to you otherwise. Aren't you glad I was able to handle him?"

Nausea filled her and she was worried about Rhodes. "I'm sorry. I meet so many people ... can you remind me of your name?"

"How can you not remember my name?" he shouted, a red flush of anger filling his face.

Oh, shit. Oh, shit. She did her best not to let her fear or panic show. "I'm sorry." She held up her hands. "I should know your name. It's..."

"Curtis." He spoke in a more even tone. "Don't make me lose my temper, Sasha. It's not good for either one of us. We've worked on three movies together. I drove you back to your trailer in Vancouver. That was our first meeting. You couldn't take your eyes off mine in the rearview mirror."

She blinked, trying desperately to remember so she didn't set off his temper again. Why would she have been looking in that mirror unless...

"The day I ended up with a black eye."

She'd had a staged fight scene and she'd ended up with an elbow to her face. She'd been so worried about bruising for filming the next day, she'd kept looking at herself in the mirror. And this man, Curtis, had taken it as interest that hadn't been there.

"Yes! I knew you'd remember our connection."

She let him keep his assumptions while she tried to find a way out of this mess. Rhodes was incapacitated, but there was still Jared and Xander who could come by any minute. She just had to keep Curtis talking.

She rubbed her palms, damp from nerves, against her slacks. "I'd like to get some air, Curtis. Can I do that?"

"No." And without warning, he pulled his hand from behind his back and revealed he was holding a serrated knife with a gleaming tip.

He walked toward her.

She stepped back and her calves hit the edge of the couch cushion. He kept coming and soon he had a hand around her waist, the knife in the other hand.

Oh, God. She bit back a sob.

"I'm going to keep the knife between us and we're

going to walk off the set. My car is right behind the trailers. Don't say a word or yell." He nudged her side with the knife to make his point.

The prick of the blade against her soft chiffon top hurt but she refused to react.

"Did you hear me?"

"Yes." She nodded, doing her best not to tremble or show fear. At the first opportunity, she would take her chances and escape.

"Then let's go."

She braced herself, but before she could take a step, the doorknob turned, making the same noise as earlier. "That's Xander. He's the only one who would just walk in." Or try to.

"Sasha?" Xander called out. "Open up. It's me."

Before she could respond, Curtis slammed a hand over her mouth, gripping her skin tightly. He covered her nose and mouth, making it hard for her to breathe.

She squirmed against him, and he reminded her of the knife by holding it against her side. She stilled immediately.

"Sasha!" Xander sounded worried.

Spots flitted in front of her eyes from lack of oxygen. Dammit, she didn't want to faint and leave Xander to deal with the crazy man on his own. She caught sight of the snack table with the water pitcher nearby.

She kicked out her foot, knocking over the table. The metal pitcher and glasses crashed to the floor, shattering and making enough noise to be heard outside.

XANDER WAS PISSED and needed to take a walk. He wasn't sure if his anger was directed at Sasha for being unable to commit to a simple weekend away or at himself for building up expectations when he knew better. She'd talked a good game about learning from the past, but when faced with a choice, she couldn't make a decision. She'd said she needed time, when in reality, she wanted to weigh all her options first and choose the best one for her career.

He wasn't so self-absorbed that he didn't understand why she needed time. But his ego, which she'd damaged once before, and his heart, which, dammit, he'd given to her again, weren't ready for the end.

"Xander."

He stopped and turned to see Jared coming his way. "Why are you here and not with Sasha?"

"Rhodes is standing guard at the trailer. I stepped away to make a call."

Xander nodded. "I'm going to head back. I'll text you when we're ready to head home."

He made his way to the trailer and Rhodes was

nowhere to be seen. No way in hell would the man take a break with Sasha inside. After the incident with Cassidy, her security, someone new to Alpha's firm, had been fired for neglecting to meet her at the door and walk her to the car. Xander had no doubt everyone involved in this situation had been warned.

He glanced around the trailer, catching sight of someone laying in the bushes across the way. Which meant Sasha was in trouble. He shot a regret-filled look at the man on the ground and pulled out his phone, hitting redial for Jared. He filled him in as he ran to check on Sasha.

He jogged up the steps and yanked on the doorknob only to find it locked. She always left it open for him when she was inside, knowing her security detail was close by.

"Sasha?" he yelled out, trying again to yank on the doorknob. "Open up. It's me."

No one answered.

Frustrated, he called out again. "Sasha!"

The sound of something crashing came from inside. Without wasting more time, he stepped back and slammed at the door with his foot. No luck. Trying again, he rammed into it with his shoulder this time, the door flying off its flimsy hinges.

He burst inside to find the same guy who'd tried to keep him off set the first day of filming standing with an arm around Sasha, a knife at her neck.

He immediately held up his hands. "Take it easy," he said to the man whose eyes were darting everywhere, sweat beading on his forehead.

Xander met Sasha's panicked gaze, trying to calm her with a look. He didn't have a clue yet how he'd get her out of this mess unharmed, but that was the only acceptable option.

"You ruined everything!" the guy said, glaring at Xander. "She was supposed to be on this set alone. I'd have her all to myself. She's mine. Mine! Do you hear me?" His hand shook and the knife pricked her skin.

She winced as Xander clenched his hands at his sides. "You don't want to hurt her," he told the man in a calm voice. "You care about her, remember? So why don't you lower the knife and–"

Before he could finish his sentence, Sasha reached behind her and did something that caused the man to shriek in pain, but he held on to her arm. She tried to yank out of his grasp, and Xander rushed forward at the same instant the asshole lunged for her, shoving her hard, away from where Xander stood.

She hadn't caught her balance from her attempted escape, and his hard push propelled her against the edge of the counter beside the couch. Her head hit the hard surface with a sickening thud.

His stomach rolled and panic filled him, but he

dove, tackling the man, shoving the knife beneath the sofa and out of his reach. He had no patience for a struggle, so he lifted his arm and punched him in the jaw over and over until his head rolled back and he was out of commission.

Xander pushed himself up and ran for Sasha. Blood pooled from the side of her head, scaring him. He yanked off his shirt, knelt down and used the material to put pressure on the wound, reminding himself that head injuries bled heavily.

He placed his free hand on her cheek. "Hey, sunshine."

She moaned and those beautiful sky blue eyes fluttered open. "Hi."

He smiled because she was conscious and he didn't want her to see how fucking frightened he was.

"Jesus!"

Xander heard Jared's voice and turned his head. "Tie up that asshole. Then call 911 and the cops," he said, heart pounding hard in his chest.

"No. I'll be fine." Sasha attempted to sit and he saw the moment she accepted defeat. He wrapped his arm around her and lowered her so her head lay in his lap and he resumed putting pressure on her wound.

She winced and he gritted his teeth. "Sorry but that head injury needs to be checked out. You're bleeding," he said, not wanting to scare her, but she did need to remain where she was.

Jared did his thing with the groaning man on the floor and then began to bark out orders on his phone.

"You did well," he told her, stroking her cheek.

"I grabbed his nuts." She tried to grin and winced instead. "Xander, I have something I need to tell you. Something interesting—"

"Shh." He placed a finger over her lips. "Talking can wait. You need your strength." From the looks of the head wound, she probably needed stitches, not to mention, she might have a concussion.

Jared strode over and knelt beside them. "Jackass is zip-tied on the floor. The cops and paramedics are on the way. What the hell happened?"

Xander gave a brief explanation, then asked, "How's Rhodes?"

"He's conscious," Jared said. "If you two are okay, I'm going to wait with him."

"Tell him I'm sorry he was hurt," Sasha said.

Jared met her gaze. "It's not your fault. He was doing his job. Sit tight until the paramedics get here," he said, then strode out of the trailer.

Xander continued to stare at the face of the woman he loved.

He stroked her cheek and whispered calming nonsensical words until the cops rushed in, the paramedics right behind them.

★ ★ ★

XANDER HAD INSISTED on accompanying Sasha to the hospital in the ambulance, and since she wouldn't let go of his hand, the paramedics agreed.

Once they arrived, they took Sasha to be examined, leaving Xander alone in the waiting room. He'd left Jared with the police, who said they would question Sasha when she was up to answering them.

While Xander paced, he called the people who needed to know what had happened to Sasha. Then he waited some more. He glanced at the clock on the wall for what felt like the gazillionth time when the outside doors opened and Cassidy ran in.

She looked flustered and afraid, and he stepped into her line of vision. "Hey, Cassidy."

"Xander, is she okay?"

"Yes," he was quick to reassure her.

She expelled a long breath of air, her relief as strong as his, and then she wrapped her arms around him and burst into tears.

Xander patted her back, feeling somewhat awkward but knowing Cassidy needed a friend.

"Hey, you two. What's going on?" Xander glanced up to see Dash standing beside them, hands in the front pockets of his jeans as he took in Cassidy. In Xander's arms.

He released her and she stepped back. She glanced

down as she opened her shoulder bag and pulled out a tissue, dabbing under her eyes. "I was worried about Sasha, and when Xander told me she would be okay, I just … lost it."

"Understandable. So Sasha will be fine?"

Xander inclined his head. "I'm waiting for details, but the paramedics said they believed she had a mild concussion and would need stitches." Just as he'd thought. But he hated that she had to suffer and was in pain. "I wish I'd shown up at the trailer sooner but…" He shook his head.

"What?" Dash asked.

"I was pissed about something and took a walk to cool off instead of staying with her." He ran a hand over his head and groaned.

Dash and Cassidy glanced at one another before she spoke up. "You can't blame yourself. This guy was determined to get to her. At least now he's no longer a threat to anyone."

Dash casually put an arm around her. "You're right. And how are you? Are you okay?"

Xander was too worked up to get into it with his brother over flirting with Cassidy. At this point, Dash appeared to be genuinely concerned, and Xander would let it go at that.

"Yes, but I want to see Sasha," she said, seemingly comforted by Dash's presence.

"Join the club," Xander muttered. He glanced at his sibling. "Thanks for coming."

"No sweat."

They made their way to the free chairs. Xander was aware of people staring at his rock-star brother, but it didn't bother him. He just sat down and pulled Cassidy into the seat next to him.

Xander picked a chair across from them and waited for news. Unfortunately, before someone came out with information, the outer doors swung open, and the last person Xander wanted to see walked in and headed straight for him.

"Where is she?" Rebecca, Sasha's barracuda agent, asked, as if she were the parent with every right to see her child.

Xander rose to his feet. "They're checking her out. We should hear something definitive any minute."

"And the bastard is under arrest?"

"Yes. Who called you?"

Rebecca rolled her eyes. "Do you think Isaac missed one of his stars being taken out by ambulance?"

"I don't know. I had bigger concerns than who was watching," Xander said. This woman always irritated the fuck out of him.

Dash rose from his seat. "Come on. Let's settle down and wait for news."

"Xander Kingston?" He spun at the sound of his name. A nurse stood by the double doors to the emergency room main entrance.

"That's me." Ignoring everyone else, he strode over to the petite woman. "How is she?"

"Good," the brunette was quick to assure him. "She's asking for you."

His heart, which had been in a static state, began to beat normally again. "I'm coming."

"Xander, make sure I get in to see her, too," Rebecca said.

He clenched his jaw but didn't answer. Instead, he followed the nurse through the doors, past a large desk and curtained cubicles.

She stopped in front of a closed striped curtain and gestured toward it. "You can go in.

He pulled back the curtain far enough so he could step inside. Sasha lay with her head against a pillow, eyes closed, the light above her turned off.

He walked forward and sat in the chair next to the bed, taking her hand in his. "Hey."

She opened her eyes slowly and met his gaze, smiling at him. "Hi."

"How bad is the pain?" Given her pale skin, he was going to assume she hurt a lot, and he wished he could take it away.

She raised one delicate shoulder beneath the hospital gown. "Not great. The doctor said I have a slight concussion. I threw up when I got here," she said, blushing.

He rubbed his thumb over the top of her hand. "Stitches?"

"No. They were able to stop the bleeding and decided I didn't need any," she said, her voice soft.

"Good."

"Xander, thank you for kicking that door down. He wanted to take me to his car and if that happened..." She shuddered at the thought.

His hand clasped hers tighter. "I shouldn't have left you alone to begin with."

"I was with Jared." She blinked and her eyes widened. "What happened to Rhodes?"

"He was knocked out. Hit pretty hard with a blunt object. Those damned trailers were so secluded it gave the stalker the edge." Xander ground his teeth at the reminder. "He's going to be okay. I got a text from Jared. Just really sore for a while."

"I feel responsible."

Of course she did. "The risk comes with his job. Don't worry about him. Just relax."

"Xander," she began.

"Rest. There's plenty of time for talk later. I just want to let Cassidy in to see you. She's beside herself. So let's reassure her you're okay." He leaned down and kissed the tip of her nose. "Close your eyes for a few minutes. I'll go get her."

"I don't care about rules. I want to see her now." Rebecca's loud voice carried through the outer room and into the cubicle.

Sasha winced. "She's here, too?"

"Isaac called her." He'd wanted to give Cassidy a few minutes alone with Sasha before her agent took over.

The curtain opened and Rebecca let herself in, a nurse standing behind her. "I'm sorry, Miss Keaton. If you want me to get security, I will."

"That's okay," Sasha said to the younger woman.

It wasn't, not as far as Xander was concerned, and he turned to glare at Sasha's agent. "You couldn't wait?" He pushed himself up from his seat.

"Sasha, are you okay?" Rebecca edged past him and walked up to the bed.

"I'll be fine," she said, her voice still softer than usual. Probably in deference to her pounding head, if his own experience with a concussion was anything to go by.

Xander stepped back and walked out, giving Sasha a few minutes with her agent. He waited outside with no intention of eavesdropping, but Rebecca's voice did not allow for private conversation.

So Xander listened as Rebecca asked questions,

but Sasha spoke too low for him to hear her reply.

"Well, I have news that's going to perk you right up," Rebecca said. "Daniel Larsen wants you for his next film."

Daniel Larsen was an A-List director with two Academy Awards under his belt. Any film he chose next was destined to follow suit, especially with the right talent. Which Sasha was.

Xander's stomach twisted so hard the pain gutted him. He was as proud of her as he was destroyed by the news.

"And guess where they are filming? Singapore!" she said, obviously before Sasha could question her. Rebecca went on, detailing the role Sasha would play and information Xander tuned out.

He stood in the outer area of the emergency room as any hope he had for the future disappeared. Sasha had been offered every actress's dream role, and he would not stand in her way. They'd had an agreement that this thing between them would end when filming did. And though he'd hoped they could make a relationship work, shame on him for thinking they could actually do it.

She was off to Singapore. Then where?

There was no way they could have a real future. A solid relationship. A family. Things he not only wanted but needed to be whole. He desired so much more than his parents had given him growing up, and no matter how much he loved her, Sasha was not the woman who could share that life with him. And since he couldn't imagine being with anyone else, he figured that left him shit out of luck.

Since he'd spaced out during the rest of their conversation, his pounding heart and thoughts drowning out everything else, he was surprised when Rebecca pushed past the curtain.

She narrowed her gaze at Xander. "She wants to see Cassidy but I'm not leaving. Sasha and I have more to discuss."

He rolled his eyes. The woman was relentless, but the fact remained, it wasn't his place to get rid of Sasha's agent so she could rest. She was an adult who would want to handle her own life.

"Stall her five minutes. I need to have a word with Sasha first."

The last word they'd have before everything changed.

Chapter Eleven

S ASHA CLOSED HER eyes, which felt much better than staring at the ceiling, waiting for someone to come in and discuss discharging her. She was overwhelmed with a mix of emotions. The fear she'd felt in the trailer had begun to subside, and the reality of her stalker being under arrest was setting in. Thank goodness.

Rebecca had stepped out, but not before insisting Sasha needed to think about her news and the opportunity before making a decision. Sasha was annoyed that her agent thought this was the right time to discuss business. After Sasha had been attacked by her stalker and was in the hospital.

But all Rebecca cared about was the fact that she was negotiating a salary and expected to nail down a multimillion-dollar deal. She'd insisted Sasha would be crazy to walk away from it, but she was crazy. Crazy in love with Xander and the life she could have with him and his big, welcoming family.

She'd been earning substantial money for approximately two years now, and with the endorsements she'd done, she was well set up for a good long while. Her choice to take a step back from acting and try her hand at establishing and running a production company had nothing to do with money, and she knew how fortunate she was to be able to say that.

Now she had to find out just how invested Xander was in a future with her. Footsteps sounded outside the curtain, and the man in question strode into the room.

"Hi," she said, still needing to keep her voice soft in deference to the pain in her skull.

"Hi."

"Where is Cassidy?" she asked.

"In the waiting room with Dash and Rebecca."

She narrowed her gaze. Rebecca hadn't left? Now that was a shock. Was she going to have to repeat herself again before her agent believed where things stood?

Xander shoved his hands into his front pants pockets and didn't meet her gaze, and a funny feeling twisted in Sasha's stomach. "Xander? What's wrong?"

He cleared his throat. "I heard your conversation with Rebecca about the new movie she's lined up for you."

Oh, no. Sasha hadn't wanted him to find out from anyone but her so she could soften the news with the plan she'd just recently come up with. "Yes but—"

Before she could explain, he rolled his shoulders back and looked her in the eye. "It's a great opportunity and the timing is perfect. You've wrapped this movie and intended to go back to California anyway."

She shook her head, a huge mistake since the pain was excruciating. "I never said what I intended to do. I was considering my options."

"And now you have one you can't turn down." He shrugged as if it were no big deal. As if her heart or his wasn't on the line here.

He remained too far from the edge of the bed, and she wished she could reach over and touch him, remind him of their connection, but he clearly didn't want that.

"Look," he began. "When we started up again, we said this thing between us was temporary. And I just want you to know I won't stand in your way. You're talented and you deserve everything you've always wanted for yourself and your career." He spoke without inflection, his tone hard, similar to the Xander he'd been when she showed up at his house a few weeks ago. The one who believed she'd always choose her career over him.

If she thought her head was hurting before, now that she was holding back tears, the physical pain was infinitely worse.

"What about us?" she asked.

Because if he didn't love her, if he could let her go so easily, without a fight, her choices had to be about herself. Not about them as a couple. Nothing she did would change. She still didn't want to go back to full-time travel and acting. A production company would still be in her plans, just in California, not New York. With him. But he'd have to tell her they were over. She needed to hear it from his mouth.

She held her breath, waiting. Praying he'd look into her eyes and understand her feelings. She wasn't going to lay her emotions bare when his mind was already made up.

"There is no us, Sasha," he said, breaking her heart. "There never was. Not long-term, anyway."

Though she'd anticipated the words, she still blinked in disbelief. "Didn't we say we were going to see what happened when the movie ended? Shouldn't we talk about possibilities for the future?"

He shook his head. "I'm going back to the beach and my quiet, peaceful life. I wish you all the best with yours." And on that comment, he turned and walked out, leaving her behind.

She held back the sob just waiting to come out until his footsteps receded and he wouldn't hear her cry. Then she let her emotions come out. Within minutes, Cassidy rushed in, and Sasha was able to cry on her best friend, which hurt like a bitch given her head injury.

"I'm going to kill him," Cassidy said. "If I hadn't been in a rush to get to you, I'd have done it in the waiting room. I'd like to twist his balls until he can't walk or fuck again," she said, patting a hiccupping Sasha on the back.

Sasha couldn't help but smile at her friend's brutal plan. "What did he say?" she asked, pulling back and laying her head on the pillow again.

Cassidy glanced her way. "That you wanted different things and I should make sure you're okay."

"Stupid, macho asshole. He wouldn't let me speak or explain. He just pronounced judgment. His decision. I shouldn't turn down a huge role. He wouldn't stand in my way. What about what I want?" she asked, tears rolling down her cheeks.

"Did you tell him you loved him and wanted to make it work?" Cassidy asked.

Sasha sniffed and grabbed for a tissue on the rolling tray beside the bed. "I reminded him that we'd agreed to discuss things when the movie ended. That I hadn't made any decision to go right back to LA, no matter what he might think."

She blew her nose, wincing at the pain in her head. "And when I asked him what about us, he said there was no us. So I wasn't about to shout *I love you* as he walked out on me in the hospital," she muttered, getting angry now at how he'd taken her choices away.

And left her again.

A WHILE LATER, Sasha had been discharged with instructions to rest, drink lots of fluids, and not to drive a car for at least forty-eight hours. Sounded fine to her. All she wanted was a dark room where she could lay her sore head on a pillow and do her best not to cry over Xander. It helped that the more time that passed, the more furious she became.

Dash took Sasha and Cassidy to the hotel where Cassidy had been staying. Sasha refused to go back to Xander's apartment to get the clothes and other things she'd left there. Though he'd said he was going to the Hamptons and Dash told her his plan had been to pick up Bella and be gone by the time she arrived, she had no desire to walk into a place that smelled so much like him and contained brief but wonderful memories.

Considering they'd showed up the same day asking, the hotel didn't have any connecting rooms open or suites available for Sasha. But they did have a room on the same floor as Cassidy. Sasha took it, refusing to stay with her friend. She wanted to be alone and Cassidy understood. She did, however, insist on a second key so she could check in on the patient throughout the night. Sasha couldn't argue when Cassidy was so worried and the discharging doctor had suggested she be looked in on.

The three of them were in Cassidy's hotel room, one king size bed in the center, Sasha sat on the edge of the bed, Dash leaned against the wall and Cassidy stood by Sasha, a worried look on her face.

Sasha couldn't help but notice that Dash was being amazing. He'd stepped up in his brother's absence. What Sasha hadn't expected was the sexual tension between Cassidy and Dash. Sure, Sasha had seen him watching her at the club last Saturday. And she'd seen his concern when Cassidy had been injured, and it was obvious he was interested.

But Dash was a man-whore. A playboy. A rock star who went through women, no doubt leaving broken hearts behind him. Xander had confirmed that the press about his brother was true, and Sasha didn't want her best friend to be among the trail of women he left in his wake. Nobody deserved to feel the hurt Sasha was currently experiencing.

Dash's phone suddenly emitted a song – one of his own, of course. His ego knew no bounds. He glanced at the screen, frowned, and began typing.

"Everything okay?" Cassidy asked.

Dash ran a hand through his sexily disheveled hair. "Just my asshole brother checking on Sasha."

She let out a growl. "Tell him if he has questions about me to ask me himself."

Dash raised an eyebrow. "Would you answer if he did?"

"No," she muttered. She needed time to process what he'd done to her. To them.

Dash returned to his texting and shoved the phone into his back pocket. "You know, despite the fact that our parents stayed married, we didn't grow up in a stable environment."

Sasha and Cassidy exchanged glances, surprised at Dash's personal revelation, though Sasha realized he was trying to tell her something about Xander.

She met Dash's gaze and nodded, encouraging him to continue.

"Our father was a cheating asshole, and he definitely didn't understand me and my music or Xander and..." Dash trailed off. "Well, I guess it was the fact that Xander didn't want to go to college or business school or work in the family business the way Linc had that pissed Dad off. They were always butting heads and that was their main interaction. Kenneth Kingston wasn't much of a father."

Sasha swallowed hard. "I know most of that. But what does it have to do with how Xander walked out on me so easily? Like everything we'd built again meant nothing." At the thought, the lump in her throat grew larger.

Cassidy, Sasha noted, watched him with soft eyes. Dammit, her friend was falling for the bad-boy rocker.

Dash groaned. "It's hard to feel like you're worth big sacrifices when you weren't supported growing up. And Xander's not like me. He's settled. Calm. Stoic. He needs peace. And ultimately, I think he wants the family we never had. I mean the man has a dog he takes everywhere. He already has the house to settle down in."

Sasha narrowed her gaze. "So do you."

Dash's mouth quirked in a slight smile. "With band members who come and go at will and frequent parties. Not the same thing."

No, it wasn't, Sasha thought, glancing at Cassidy, who wouldn't meet her gaze.

"If I had to guess, in Xander's eyes, he thinks you're like me."

Sasha's own eyes opened wide at that pronouncement. "I'm sorry, what?"

"You travel from country to country or within the States for whichever movie comes next. The paparazzi follow us both with flashing lights and cameras, trying to dig into our personal lives. Not to mention ... a stalker." He gestured to her head. "He knows himself well enough to understand it's too much for him—for Xander the veteran and the man. And he didn't want to make you choose between your career and him. So he did it for you."

"You're very intuitive," Sasha murmured.

He shrugged. "I can read my brother pretty well. Better than myself."

She bit down on her bottom lip, waiting for Dash to continue and to finally make his point. So far she'd gleaned that her life wasn't what his brother wanted.

"He never gave me the chance to tell him I'm finished with living that way, that I have a plan for my future that includes him. He just blew off what we shared and left."

Dash looked at her with understanding in his gaze. "Because he'd rather walk away first than have you reject him. Keep in mind, this really is armchair psychology. It's what I see when I watch Xander and how he acted with you."

She sighed, the sound deep, from inside her chest. "I understand but I'm furious. I deserve better. He should have manned up and told me how he feels about me. He should have let me tell him what *I* need."

"You're right. And I'm betting he'll come to that same conclusion pretty soon."

Or he wouldn't. Who knew. He'd taken her off guard today, and she wasn't certain what was going on in that thick-headed brain of his.

A part of her wanted to head to the Hamptons now and give him a piece of her mind, something she should have done at the hospital, but she'd been blindsided and concussed. She'd have to give herself a pass. And right now, she felt like utter crap and needed a nap.

"Thanks, Dash. For everything." She turned to Cassidy. "Can we talk?" She gestured for them to go out into the hall.

Her friend nodded. "Sure. I'll walk you to your room."

Dash flopped down on the bed, bracing his hands behind his head and leaning against the headboard. "I'll be waiting when you get back."

Dammit, Sasha thought. She grasped Cassidy's elbow and walked her to the door, opened it, set the security latch so Cassidy could get back in, and let the door swing almost shut behind them.

"What are you doing?" she asked her friend in a harsh whisper. "That man is going to rip your heart out."

"Shh!" Cassidy's eyes opened wide. "And no, he won't. I'm not invested that way. It's just fun for now."

Sasha folded her arms across her chest and narrowed her gaze. "Your brother wouldn't think so."

"Axel is not going to find out unless someone tells

him. Besides, I'm a grown woman. He can't dictate who I sleep with."

Sasha's mouth parted. "I knew it! You already did it!"

A red flush rose to Cassidy's cheeks. "Not yet but I intend to." She nudged Sasha lightly with her shoulder. "Come on. I'm on the rebound and I need this. Besides, when will I get a chance with a man as hot as Dash Kingston ever again?"

"You should look in the mirror, Cass. You're beautiful. Any guy would be lucky to have you. And I've seen how you look at him. You're smitten already."

"Don't be ridiculous." She waved her hand, dismissing the possibility. "I know what I'm doing. Now let's get you into bed so you can rest. Something tells me you're going to need energy to deal with *your* Kingston brother."

She smirked and put a hand on Sasha's shoulder. "It's not over, Sasha. You just need to get Xander to open up."

She frowned, unsure about everything. "We'll see. Right now, I'm still furious at him for leaving me at the hospital and upset he didn't fight for us."

Cassidy's expression grew soft with understanding. "So don't make it easy for him. But one way or another, I have faith you two will work out."

Sasha wasn't as sure.

★　★　★

XANDER WOKE UP hungover, his mouth tasting like cotton, his head pounding, and his dog licking his face. A glance at the clock told him he'd missed walking her at a reasonable time. No wonder she was antsy.

"Sorry, girl," he said as he dragged his ass out of bed. Even his voice sounded like he'd eaten rocks. God knows how much tequila he'd had to drink last night when he'd drowned his sorrows so he didn't have to think about how badly he'd fucked up with Sasha.

He grabbed his glasses, knowing his vision was going to be fuzzy today, and put them on. After a quick bathroom trip, he unset the alarm and headed to the sliding glass doors to the backyard, letting Bella out before he had a problem on his hands. He left the door open so she could come back in on her own and walked to the kitchen to make himself a cup of coffee.

Although he wished he could stop replaying yesterday in his head, the memory went round and round in a never-ending loop. He'd heard Rebecca's offer and immediately reverted to their past, when Sasha had been so immersed in starting her career, she'd chosen co-stars and roles over him and their relationship.

With distance and a whole lot of alcohol, he knew damn well that while he'd been standing outside the curtain listening to her agent offer her the world, he'd jumped the gun and ended things before she could pick her career over him again.

Abandoning her while she was in the hospital and when she needed him was a dick move. Hell, he wouldn't blame her if she never spoke to him again.

His stomach lurched at the thought just as his Keurig spurted the caffeinated hot drink into the mug. He poured some milk and took a long sip just as the alarm beeps on his door let him know someone had entered. Xander didn't need to guess who'd let himself in, and he prepared himself to deal with Dash.

"Hey, asshole."

With a groan, Xander met his brother's gaze. "How is she?"

"Physically she's in some pain and exhausted. Emotionally, I think she moved pretty quickly from devasted to pissed as hell. What the fuck were you thinking?" Dash walked into the kitchen, pushed Xander out of the way, and made himself a mug of coffee.

"I think we can agree that I wasn't. Not rationally, anyway."

While waiting for the coffee to drip, he took in Xander's appearance. "You look like shit."

"I overdid the tequila last night." He took a long sip of the hot coffee while Dash lifted his out of the machine and poured milk into the mug.

"Do you have a plan?"

Xander shook his head. "I just woke up and faced what I did. I can't believe I fucking panicked."

Dash drank his coffee and studied him. "You and I both had a shit relationship with Dad. I mean, we all did, but we were the ones he didn't understand or approve of. And I think those issues, added to the crappy way he treated Mom, left scars. In my case, I don't do relationships, and even when I don't mean to, I fuck up what could be a good thing."

Xander narrowed his gaze, wondering if that comment had something to do with Cassidy. Because Dash wasn't in a confessing mood and this lecture was more for Xander's sake, he didn't ask.

"And in your case, the one time you tried, she trampled on your heart." Before Xander could give his own input, Dash raised a hand. "Ignore the sappy way this is coming out. My point is, I know you bailed before she could crush you again." He lifted his mug to his lips, took a drink, and swallowed. "And don't kick my ass or anything but I told Sasha as much."

Xander leaned against the counter and accepted that Dash had his best interests at heart. And if he could soften Sasha before Xander talked to her, all the better.

He placed his mug on the counter and groaned. "I

can't get it right. The first time around, I expected way too much from someone so young and trying to build a career, and this time, in bending so far the other way so I wouldn't repeat the same mistake, I pushed her away." Though he couldn't deny Dash's point. Protecting himself played a large role. "I was an ass."

"Can't argue that point." Dash put his coffee next to Xander's. "But I was worse if that makes you feel any better."

Xander shook his head. "I told you to stay the hell away from Cassidy. What'd you do?"

Dash raised an eyebrow. "I'm taking the Fifth. I don't want you to have to haul off and hit me."

Xander ran a hand over his face and groaned. Reading between the lines, he figured his brother had slept with her and bailed the morning after. He'd lecture him but his own behavior wasn't much better. "Fine. I'd rather not know, anyway."

Dash looked away, obviously lost in thought, and whatever was going on between him and Sasha's best friend, Xander figured he was better off staying out of it.

"I need a favor," he said.

Dash glanced at him. "Name it."

"Take Bella?" He pointed to the dog, who was chowing down on her breakfast that had been left in the bowl. She was a grazer, eating when she felt like it and not at set times. "I need to go to the city and I don't want to leave her alone."

Dash had a stash of her food and bowls at his house, too, so Xander didn't have to worry if he was gone overnight.

"Going to make it up to your girl?" Dash asked.

Xander rolled his stiff shoulders. "Something tells me she's not my girl anymore," he said, not bothering to hide his anger at himself.

"You can be charming when you want to be. And if all else fails, grovel." Dash chuckled and called for Bella, who'd stopped eating, had taken a drink from her bowl, and was lying on the floor watching them.

Xander grabbed a leash that hung from a hook by the door and handed it to his brother. Dash clipped the hook to Bella's collar and Xander knelt, taking her doggy face between his hands. "Be good for Dash. Don't crap in the house and sleep in your bed there." He kissed her nose and stood. "Don't let any of your bandmates feed her human food or alcohol," he said.

Dash crossed his chest over his heart with his index finger. "I've got her. Don't worry."

They walked to the front door and Xander pulled it open. "You think Axel will work out with the band?"

Dash nodded. "I really do. We did some riffing and we gelled. I think we can work something out with him. PR will have to come up with a plan to announce that he's joining the Original Kings. I'm amped up about it."

"That's great. At least you didn't have to have a huge talent search, except..." Xander trailed off, wondering if he should say what he was thinking.

"I fucked his sister?" Dash said it for him, causing Xander to wince.

"Really? You have to talk like that and treat her like any other groupie?" Xander was pissed on Cassidy's behalf and Sasha would lose her mind.

Dash shook his head, looking embarrassed. "I'm trying to convince myself that's all it was to me," he admitted. "A typical night."

"But it wasn't?" Xander braced a hand on the doorframe.

"She's special. But I'm ... me. And she knows that." He stepped outside and Bella trotted along with him.

Xander groaned. He and Dash might be different, but in fucking up potential relationships, they had too much in common.

He shut the door behind them and leaned against it, debating his options. First up was a shower. No run this morning unless he wanted to end up with a migraine courtesy of the hangover that was already killing his head. Then he had the long ride to the city to figure out what he'd say to Sasha.

He understood that even if he groveled, as Dash suggested, told her he loved her and wanted forever, she might tell him she was taking the role in Singapore. But at least he'd apologize, attempt to win her back, and most importantly, give her a say about her future.

By breaking things off, he'd taken her choices away. And given how pushy both her mother and agent were, he should have known better than to tell her what was best for her. Sasha ought to make those decisions for herself. Even if he was the one hurt in the end. Amazing what a bottle of tequila and a night of drunk talking to himself would accomplish.

Throughout last night, he'd weighed his options. Not always easy when drunk, but he did his best. And when it came down to losing Sasha for good or dealing with her career, in whatever form she wanted it to take, he'd decided to deal. Fuck it all. He would cope with the paparazzi, the travel, the fans, all of it if he could have Sasha in his life.

If he had to visit his old therapist and work out leftover stress and PTSD issues from his time abroad, he would do it. Anything to make *them* work. Now he just had to apologize and convince her that this time would be different.

Plan in mind, he showered, dressed, and headed out.

His car was parked in front of the house, and he opened the door to find Sasha, her hand in the air about to ring the doorbell.

Chapter Twelve

S ASHA PULLED HER sunglasses off and Xander immediately saw how exhausted she was. She had dark circles under her eyes and her mouth was drawn tight. He had no doubt she was in pain.

All the apologies he had planned fled in the wake of seeing her hurting. "What the hell are you doing here? You shouldn't have been on such a long car ride with a concussion," he grumbled, pulling her inside.

"I closed my eyes and rested on the way here," she said defensively.

"Is that why you look like you're about to fall over?"

"I was too pissed off to wait until I felt better." She glared at him, her anger at him massive.

He deserved every bit of it.

Thanks to him, they might be technically broken up and she might not want him to touch her, but fuck it. He'd do what he needed to. After kicking the door closed, he picked her up and settled her in his arms.

"Xander, what are you doing?" she asked, but she wrapped her arms around his neck to hold on.

Without answering, he carried her down the hall and into the master bedroom, placing her gently onto the mattress. "Kick off your shoes, lie back, and rest. I'll be right back."

Turning, he strode to the kitchen to get an ice pack and Aleve for her head and a glass of apple juice and a box of graham crackers in case she was hungry.

Then he headed back to the bedroom and braced himself for the fight of his life. Because he planned to do everything he could to convince Sasha they had what it took to make things work for the long haul.

SASHA HAD INTENDED to show up and give Xander hell, not to be the one being yelled at and carried to bed. Of course, she understood his reasoning, but his reaction put her at a disadvantage and made her look weak. But with her head pounding and nausea threatening courtesy of both the concussion and the car ride, that's what she was.

When he returned to the bedroom with juice, a snack, and medicine for her head, her heart thawed a bit, and she got angry all over again.

"No. You are not going to get out of what you did by being nice to me now." She folded her arms across her chest, and instead of feeling like she was in control, she felt like a petulant child.

Damn him.

He placed everything on the nightstand and sat down on the side of the bed, not asking her to move over, just letting his hips push her legs aside.

He was really pissing her off and she growled at him. His lips twitched and she knew he was holding back a laugh because they weren't in a place where anything was funny.

He placed one of his big, warm hands on her legging-clad thigh. She'd borrowed clothing from Cassidy since her stuff was still at his apartment.

"Sasha, listen … I was on my way to see you."

That statement took her by surprise. "Well, I came all the way out here and I want to have my say first."

He nodded. "Okay. Talk to me," he said, but he didn't move his hand from her leg, distracting her in all sorts of ways she didn't want to think about. Like the heat between her legs. How damp her sex had grown since he'd picked her up and she'd smelled his familiar, masculine scent.

She cleared her throat and met his gaze. "I think there are a few things you forgot about," she said, drawing on the many times she'd practiced this speech on the way over here so she didn't forget anything. "For one thing, I'm an adult. And I'm not the same person you met five years ago. I've grown up and taken charge of my life. So I did not appreciate you telling me what I should do. Nobody makes my life choices anymore except me. And this time around, they're well thought out with a plan behind them."

She didn't miss the way his gaze softened behind those sexy glasses as he listened. Or the way he nodded while she spoke. "Are your head or eyes bothering you today?" she couldn't help but ask.

He nodded. "Both. A little too much tequila last night."

She raised her eyebrows, surprised. Normally he wasn't a big drinker, so maybe he'd been as upset as she'd been.

But she didn't want to get further distracted. "Back to my point. You made assumptions. I never said I was going right back to California. I never said I was going to jump into another role. And I sure as hell never gave you any indication that, despite our agreement to begin a short-term affair, that's what we'd ended up being to one another." She paused for a deep breath and to let her head, which pounded harder the more worked up she got, relax a bit. She leaned her head against the pillow and sighed.

Without saying a word, he reached over, picked up the Aleve bottle from the nightstand, shook out pills, and handed them to her along with the juice.

"Thank you." She took the medicine because whatever she'd taken early this morning had worn off.

"At the very least, you owed me a two-way conversation before walking out on me *in the hospital*."

A flush rose to his cheekbones. "You're one-hundred-percent right. I was wrong and I realized it about three drinks in last night. Probably even before then but I was shaken up," he admitted. "I heard Rebecca offer you the role. I heard the destination. You were talking so quietly I couldn't make out what you were saying, but I made up my own narrative based on the past and complete fear you'd dump me and not look back."

She shook her head. "Xander, when we were together this time, we weren't the same people. We communicated with each other. We talked. I thought we were building something solid this time around."

"But when I asked you to go away with me, you couldn't give me an answer—"

"But—"

He held up a hand. "I realized afterwards what I asked for was ridiculous, leaving the same day. You had things to deal with first. But I'd had Rebecca needling me about screwing up your life, your mother pushing on her end, and my own insecurities screwing with my head."

He picked up her hand and held it between his. "I let myself return to the past. In the back of my mind was the way I grew up. How shitty my dad treated my mom and how she always let him instead of having the guts to walk out. And I didn't want to do the same thing and repeat my past mistakes. I just wanted to protect myself from ever being hurt again."

"So you ended things first." Exactly what Dash had told her.

"Yeah. Except I then had a two-hour drive here in traffic to realize I was hurting anyway." One hand held hers; the other absently rubbed his chest. "And this time I'd done it to myself," he said.

Technically he'd done it last time, too. He'd broken up with her then as well, Sasha thought. But she'd deserved it the first go-round. She hadn't taken his feelings into consideration too many times. Now things were different. Or she'd thought they were.

He met her gaze. "I also hurt you, and I'm so sorry." His contrite expression told her so much about his feelings but nothing about the future.

She sighed, a lot of the anger she'd felt deflating in the face of his heartfelt explanation and apology, but her heart was still bruised because too many things remained unresolved.

"Listen, I made some decisions that you should know about," she said, shifting herself back against the pillows until she was more comfortable. "And you would have known yesterday if you'd stuck around or at least listened to what I had to say."

He watched her warily. "Go on."

"I turned down the role, and when Rebecca came back in to see me again after you left, pushing harder, I fired her." His shocked expression was priceless but she wasn't finished. "If she could push me to make a decision on a huge new deal while I was in the hospital with a concussion, after being attacked, she does not have my best interests at heart."

"Amen," he muttered.

She would have smirked but she was still mad at him. "I told you at one point, just like I told Cassidy before we came to New York, that I was tired and the acting and travel and constant jump from role to role wasn't what I wanted. The idea of being a famous actress was instilled in me by my mother from such a young age, I never considered the downside or what else I might want to do. I didn't have a life, and being with you cemented the fact that I want one."

She curled her hand more tightly around his.

Meanwhile, he was watching her carefully, taking in her words and her expressions. She sensed his coiled tension and surprise. They'd had so much to talk about and no conclusions had been reached yet.

But she was getting there. It just remained to be seen if he was on board.

"What about your mother?" he asked.

"I called her this morning. She hit the roof, as expected. I actually feel sorry for the friends she's with on vacation. But she'll process and come around eventually. As much as I hate to say it, she needs me."

"Your money?" he asked through gritted teeth.

"In part. But she loves me, too. Once she faces that I'm serious about my plans, she'll come around."

Xander leaned in close. "And what are those plans, Sasha?"

THEY HAD TALKED about a shit ton of things in the last half hour, but a lot still remained unsaid, and Xander was about to lose his mind if she didn't get to her main point soon. So he could tell her exactly what he'd been going to New York to say.

So far she'd shocked him with everything that had come out of her mouth. Turning down the role? He'd never imagined it was possible. Firing Rebecca? Holy shit. And letting her mother know told him she was definitely serious.

"I want to start a production company. I came up with the idea yesterday, but in my gut, I know it's a good one." She glanced at him and went on. "Everything about this idea works. It will satisfy my creativity, I can act in select films if I want, and I have the contacts to reach the right people, so I'll have access to A-list talent. I can do this," she said, her voice rising with enthusiasm, and his own heart began to beat harder in his chest.

He loved seeing her excited about a project, and though this one was huge… "I have absolute faith you can pull this off."

"Well, I'll need a partner. Not for the money per se, but someone with the ability to pick a good script. Someone I trust implicitly." She raised her eyebrows as she met his gaze. "If you hadn't been such a dumb ass, making stupid choices and assumptions for me, I might have asked you. Considering I love you and all. But…"

Her lips lifted upward in a grin and Xander had had enough talk. He pulled himself over her and shut her up with a kiss. A long, deep, soul-searching kiss. One that let her know he caught what she'd said and reciprocated a hundredfold.

Lifting his head, he looked into her eyes. "I love you, too, though I would have done a more emotional job of letting you know if I'd gone first." He winked at her because he didn't give a shit how she'd told him. As long as she'd said the words.

"I was coming to the city to tell you that I was an ass, I'm sorry, and I love you." He rubbed his nose along hers before lifting his head to continue. "If I had to travel to places like Singapore to see you during filming, I'd damn well do it. I'd walk a red carpet, deal with the made-up shit in the tabloids, learn how to cope with the crowds and the flashing lights. Anything as long as I could have you."

Her eyes were damp and opened wide. "I don't know what to say. You were willing to live a life you hated ... for me?"

"Yeah," he said, his voice gruff. "Even one night knowing I'd lost you was too long. So now that you know that, I have to ask. Do you want the role? Do you want to continue on as you have been? Because you can do it and I won't go anywhere. I won't lose faith or trust in you." They'd both grown up a lot since their first attempt at a relationship.

He held his breath, waiting for her answer. Because though he'd do it, her production company idea appealed to him so much more. But this decision had to be hers.

She shook her head. "I made my choice before I came here. Even if we didn't end up together, I'm going ahead with my plan. It's definitely what I want to do."

He grinned, so fucking relieved. Well, partially relieved. "Can you work from here? Do you want to? Or is your heart set on going home?"

She shook her head. "California was never home. I bought a house but I wasn't there enough to make it mine." She placed her hands on either side of his face.

"You're my home, Xander, as long as you'll have me."

"Just try and get rid of me. And I promise you, I'll never leave you again."

He leaned down and pressed his lips to hers again, delving into her mouth but keeping her head still and being as gentle as possible because of her concussion. She bit down on his bottom lip and he groaned. He lifted his head and grinned. "You're not going to get me to do anything more. You need to rest."

"I really do. I didn't sleep well last night. I'm not used to being alone."

He rolled over and pulled her into him, wrapping his body around hers. "Then it's a good thing you'll never have to be alone again."

They lay cuddled together, everything finally right in his world. And he planned to spend the rest of his days making certain everything was perfect in hers, as well.

One Month Later…

XANDER INVITED HIS family over for a barbeque. Knowing his plan, he gritted his teeth and called Sasha's mother, offering to pay for a round-trip flight to New York and a hotel in East Hampton. She was still kicking up a fight over her daughter's choices, but Xander laid out the facts: Come and be a part of their family or remain home and start out Sasha's life with Xander on the outside looking in. Needless to say, she was staying in a hotel under the guise of wanting to visit her daughter. Xander had asked Chloe and Beck to pick Annika up on their way over.

Xander patted his jeans pocket, making sure his prized possession was where it was supposed to be, and pushed aside his nerves. He'd know when the time was right.

"Hey!" Sasha walked into the kitchen wearing a sexy sundress that revealed her bare, tanned shoulders and a tiny heart necklace he'd bought her around her neck.

She walked over and wrapped her arms around him and pressed that soft body against his firm one. He immediately grew hard against her.

"Xander, your family will be here any minute." But she didn't step away. Instead, she hugged him tighter. "This morning was amazing," she whispered in his ear.

He groaned because it so fucking was. He closed his eyes, remembering her climbing up his body, settling her legs on either side of his head, and letting him feast until she was writhing and coming hard and fast. And when she'd finished her climax, he'd urged her to slide back over him. He'd grasped her hips and thrust up inside her, finding home.

"Stop that!" She pushed his shoulder, taking him

out of his hot memory.

"What?"

"I know that look. You're thinking about sex," she said, laughing.

"You're standing in front of me looking gorgeous. Of course I am."

"Well, we have company coming." She stepped out of his grasp. "Did I tell you the good news? I spoke to Harrison Dare. He's an actor friend of mine and he's interested in talking to us about our company. We have to line up a head of development so you don't have to give up your writing to find scripts, head of production, post production and distribution. Harrison has contacts that outshine mine, believe me."

"Great. I'm looking forward to meeting him."

Sasha walked to the fridge and began to pull out food they'd ordered in and chilled. Xander had hired a catering company to clean up so they didn't have to deal with it or leave it for his housekeeper on Monday, two days from now. The two women were outside, setting up the table. They needed more room now because Dash's band members were joining them.

"I wish Linc and Jordan could come. I'm worried about her," Xander said.

Sasha nodded. "The doctor prescribed bedrest because of early cramping and contractions but he isn't worried. The longer they can keep the baby inside her, the stronger his or her lungs will be. But it's thirty-six weeks. If she goes into labor, the baby will be fine." She put a hand on his shoulder. "We could have stalled a family barbeque, you know. Until she had the baby."

He shook his head. "Linc understands about us holding it anyway."

Before she pushed him for more of an explanation, the beeps of the alarm indicated the front door had opened, and he blew out a relieved breath. "Someone's here."

"I'll go see who's arrived," she said.

He needed a minute and took a deep breath. Since they'd straightened things out between them, every-thing had fallen into place so easily it was almost scary. The stalker situation had been resolved. The man was in jail and the district attorney and his public defender were arguing over whether or not the man was sane. As long as he was locked up somewhere, Xander and Sasha were relieved.

And life had gone on. In the time since he and Sasha had gotten back together, she'd moved quickly. She'd wrapped up her life in California with incredible speed, tasking a Realtor to sell her house and help her mother find a reasonable place of her own. Cassidy had decided to move to New York where her brother also now lived. She agreed to work for Sasha and

Xander at the production company they planned to call K-Talent, for Keaton and Kingston.

Sasha had moved in with Xander, and Cassidy was staying in the house her brother was renting while she decided where she wanted to live.

Dash and Cassidy avoided each other, and when they were stuck in the same room, their behavior made it obvious something had happened between them. Sasha hadn't gotten much information out of her friend. No more than Xander had from his brother.

According to Sasha, Cassidy thought Dash was a man-whore, and she wasn't wrong. His brother enjoyed the rock-star lifestyle. Xander just wished he hadn't hurt someone so close to Sasha. It made life hard. It was a miracle Cassidy's brother, now an official part of the band, hadn't found out.

Xander heard the sound of voices and headed out to greet his family. A couple of hours later, everyone was laughing and having a good time.

Sasha, Cassidy, and Aurora had their heads together to discuss the charity project they wanted to work on, and his mother was holding nine-month-old Leah. Sasha's mother was talking to Beck's parents, who had joined them this time, along with his brothers. His father had had colon cancer but was doing well and they'd accepted the invitation.

Xander walked over and pressed a kiss to his

mom's cheek. "I'm sorry it's been so long since I've been over but we're more settled now. I promise to see you more often."

His mother, always put together and beautiful, smiled as she held Leah over her shoulder and patted the baby's back. "I know. I can't tell you how thrilled I am that you and Sasha are back together and happy. It makes my heart so full to know three of my children are settled."

She knew he planned to ask Sasha to marry him soon and was keeping his secret. But she couldn't wait and smiled wide when she looked at him. "The family rumor mill says you almost blew it with her." His mom winked.

Xander rolled his eyes. No doubt Dash had told someone, who'd told someone else, and so on. "All's well that ends well," he said, patting his pocket.

"Quit it with that move or Sasha's going to figure out you've got something going on," Dash said as he joined them.

Their mother looked at him, concern on her face. "Sarah Jenkins called this morning. Apparently there are photographs of you with your arms around two women at a strip club on social media."

Xander winced. The last person an adult man wanted to be lectured by about his sex life was his mother.

"An old friend was getting married. I posed for a picture with two women. They were fans," Dash muttered.

"Two strippers. Not that I'm passing judgment," his mother said, "but really? Must it all be so public?" she asked.

Xander glanced at his brother, who flushed beneath their mother's gaze. "It was platonic, Mom. I swear. Scout's honor." He held up his fingers. Xander wouldn't know if that was a Scout sign or not.

"You were never a Boy Scout, Dash."

"He still isn't," Xander added helpfully, which earned him a jolt in the arm.

Their mother merely shook her head.

And now seemed like the perfect time for a distraction. Xander looked across the pool area to where one of the servers was standing and nodded her way.

A little while later, everyone around the pool had a glass of champagne in their hands, except Xander and Sasha, who he'd pulled over to him in an attempt to separate her from everyone.

"I don't understand. What's going on?" she asked, glancing at everyone, who'd grown silent. And who were watching the two of them standing by the pool.

Chloe, the designated photographer, had her phone camera in her hand. She inclined her head, letting him know she was ready.

"Xander?" Sasha asked again, because he hadn't answered her.

Instead, he put his hand in his front jeans pocket, pulled out the ring, and enclosed it in his hand before dropping down to one knee.

"Xander?" Sasha asked, except she then gasped and put her hands over her mouth as she saw the four-carat ring in his hand.

The beautiful actress-turned-producer love of his life deserved nothing less. "There's a quote by an author that is perfect for us. 'A second chance doesn't mean anything if you don't learn from your first.'" The saying was attributed to Zig Ziglar, a veteran, salesman, motivational speaker, and more. "We suffered and we learned. And now I don't want to spend another minute without you by my side." He'd decided to keep it short and sweet. "I love you and need you. Sasha Keaton, will you marry me and become a Kingston?"

SASHA STARED AT the elegant ring that sparkled in the sunlight. Her family and Xander's stood around them, waiting, along with the man she adored, for her answer.

"You must be pretty confident to do this in front of everyone." Her smile grew wider as she met his gaze. "Yes, I will marry you. I love you, Xander. Then, now, and forever."

Around them, the families clapped and cheered as Xander slipped the ring on her finger.

"It fits perfectly." She blinked and happy tears dripped down her cheeks.

"I borrowed one of your rings and took it with me to the jeweler." He rose to his feet, and she threw her arms around him, pressing her lips to his.

The kiss went on and on, their tongues slipping and sliding against each other's until someone called out, "Get a room!"

Laughing, they broke apart, still staring into each other's eyes and smiling.

Sasha couldn't tear her stare from Xander and his scruffy beard and the happy grin on his handsome face. For all they'd been through, this had been worth waiting for.

She was so grateful they'd given each other just one more chance because now they had forever.

Epilogue

And another month later...

THE WAITING ROOM of the hospital was full with the entire Kingston clan waiting for Jordan to give birth. Her parents, Tamara and Patrick, were beside Xander's mom as they alternately talked and paced.

Xander sat beside Sasha, holding her hand. They'd been playing musical chairs with the rest of his siblings and significant others for the better part of three hours. Xander had talked to everyone, and he now just wanted some quiet time with Sasha.

"If it was us, would you want to know if the baby was a boy or a girl?" she asked.

He met her gaze, surprised by the question. They'd talked about everything and anything ... except having children. "I don't know. I haven't given it any thought." He paused, then asked, "Do you *want* kids?"

He held his breath. He'd always desired a family, but he hadn't thought about kids since he and Sasha had gotten engaged. He'd been too busy enjoying her. But now that the subject was on the table, he did not want her to take the possibility away from them.

"Of course I do," she said softly, squeezing his hand tight. "I want a little boy who looks like his daddy," she murmured.

He grinned. "How about a girl with Mom's blond hair and both of our blue eyes?"

She nodded, obviously happy with the idea. "But not quite yet, okay? I need time with you for a while. I want to build a solid foundation before we bring children into the mix."

He nodded, in total agreement. "I also want you to have the time you need to establish our production company and fulfill your dream." She'd spent too much time trying to succeed so her mother could validate her own existence.

"Xander, I wouldn't put this career over us having a family any more than I would have chosen acting over us being together again. We're a team. We'll build a business, and when we're ready, whenever that is, we'll have kids." She pushed herself up and kissed his lips before settling into the chair beside him again.

He wrapped an arm around her and pulled her against him, glancing up at the clock. Poor Linc. He must be losing his mind watching his wife in pain. The family had been here for three hours, but Linc and Jordan had been here for twenty hours now.

About forty minutes later, Linc stepped into the

room, looking as exhausted as he was exhilarated. "It's a boy!"

The room broke out in applause, whoops, and yells of congratulations. Everyone rose and shouted questions at him at once until Linc finally shushed everyone, raising his hands and indicating everyone should quiet down. No doubt Linc had to pull strings to get them all to be allowed to wait as it was.

"He's healthy. Eight pounds, nine ounces and twenty inches long," Linc said proudly.

"Oh, God, that's a big baby," Sasha muttered, causing Xander to chuckle and hug her in reassurance.

"What's his name?" their mom asked.

"Jasper," Linc said, still grinning.

"I love it!" Basically everyone said a version of the same thing and Xander chuckled.

"Can I see my daughter and grandson?" Tamara asked.

Xander stopped paying attention and glanced at Sasha. "Want to congratulate Linc and head home? There's too many people here to get in to see them tonight."

Sasha nodded. "We'll make arrangements to visit when Jordan says it's okay."

Xander turned to see Dash hugging a wall near the back corner of the room. "Give me a minute?"

Her gaze landed on his brother and she nodded.

"Of course."

Xander headed over to Dash, who was shifting from foot to foot. "What's going on?"

Dash shook his head. "Nothing."

"Bullshit." For a guy who was usually the life of the party and the loudest, happiest guy in the room, Dash was subdued. And it had nothing to do with the new addition to the family.

When Dash remained silent, Xander put a hand on his shoulder. "Do not make me beat it out of you in front of everyone. Talk to me. I'm here for you."

Dash glanced up at him with glazed eyes, like he hadn't slept in days. "Don't judge me. And I don't want to fucking hear it was bound to happen one day."

Now Xander was worried. "Sounds like you're doing enough of that to yourself."

Dash inclined his head and spoke so low Xander had to lean close to hear. "Some woman claims I'm the father of her baby."

Thanks for reading! Dash Kingston and Cassidy Forrester are up next in JUST ONE SPARK!

JUST ONE SPARK EXCERPT

A COUPLE OF months ago, Dash Kingston been living the dream. He'd had women at his beck and call. More money than he'd ever dreamed of earning doing something he loved. Bandmates who were his best friends, and success beyond his wildest dreams. He still had those things but also he had a huge weight sitting on his chest in the form of an outstanding paternity test, courtesy of one night with a woman he barely remembered, and whose name he hadn't known at the time.

Word had spread over social media, television entertainment and celebrity news, and whatever magazines still showed up in grocery store check-out lines. Instead of talk about the band's music and their new drummer, Axel Forrester, there was speculation about whether The Original Kings' lead singer had impregnated a one night stand.

Talk about a wake up call.

Dash glanced around his patio where clusters of people gathered talking. The professionals stood on one side, the roadies and groupies, the women who wanted to fuck a rock star, laughed and partied on the other. His band members were scattered around, all having fun on a hot, late September day in East Hampton, with the alcohol at Dash's expense.

Whose idea was a party when his entire world might be falling apart? He ran a hand through his hair and decided to head over to his brother, Xander's house, about a mile down the road. Though he could walk, he took his baby, a Ferrari, Limited Edition V12 supercar. Not even the power of the engine or the yellow racing stripe he loved, helped his mood.

On the short ride, he thought about the many mistakes he'd made in life and decided he could do better. And though he knew if the kid was his, he'd step up, he prayed to God he'd dodge this bullet. Panic induced sweat broke out on his skin and he pumped up the air conditioner.

When he arrived at Xander's, his other brother, Linc's car sat in the driveway. So he'd have both brothers to hang out with. Dash let himself inside and heard their voices coming from the kitchen.

He walked into the huge room where Linc and Xander were sitting at the table. "Hey."

They looked up when he entered. "How are you holding up?" Linc asked.

Dash strode to the refrigerator, opened the door and took out a can of Diet Coke. "Feeling like shit." He popped the top and guzzled a long sip.

"How long until you have news?" Xander asked.

"My lawyer should call me any minute. Hour. Day. Fuck!" He raised a hand and caught himself, not wanting to hit anything in his brother's kitchen. Or break his hand on the granite countertops.

Xander and Linc exchanged knowing looks.

"Come on. Sit." Xander strode over, hooked an arm around Dash's neck and pulled him towards the chairs by the table. Releasing him, which Dash appreciated because he was choking, Xander then braced both palms on his shoulders and pushed until Dash dropped into the chair.

"Look, I'd be as crazy as you are if it was happening to me but right now the best thing you can do is calm the fuck down," Xander said.

"I know." And he did but was it possible? Hell, no.

Linc shook his head. "I hope this goes without saying but once you survive this scare, things need to change."

Dash did his best not to scowl or punch his brother for thinking now was a good time for life lectures.

"Linc, chill, yeah?" Xander gave Linc a pointed look.

"I'm just looking out for him," Linc said, leaning back in his chair, always the composed brother.

"I know you are." Dash got where Linc was coming from. He'd also noticed Linc had said *when* Dash survived this scare. Not if. Which meant his oldest sibling had faith Dash might get through this unscathed. Not be a father. Dash just hoped Linc was right.

Since their dead father hadn't been a good parent, Linc had always felt the need to herd the rest of the siblings and make sure they were taken care of. Whether they needed his guidance or not. Dash didn't blame him. Hell, he appreciated his oldest brother. He just wasn't in the mood for a lecture.

He was damned lucky the woman in question was willing to do a noninvasive DNA test. A blood sample from mom, one from dad, and a fetal cell analysis, would provide a result that was ninety nine percent accurate. The fact that the chick was willing to do one told Dash she wasn't a money hungry whore.

If he'd knocked her up, he wouldn't marry her but she and the baby wouldn't want for a damned thing, and Dash would get to know his kid. His stomach cramped at the notion of having a baby with a stranger.

"Are the guys at your place?" Xander asked.

The question shook Dash from his disturbing thoughts. "They were out by the pool when I left."

Xander folded his arms across his chest. "Any chance I'll have a houseful of people soon?" he asked, not sounding happy about it.

"You never know." Dash couldn't stop the grin lifting the corners of his mouth at Xander's predictable rection.

Dash had made it his life's mission to drive his more solitary brother crazy by showing up uninvited, all the time. Xander was uptight and could use a good shaking up. But despite it all, they were close.

Now that Xander lived with his fiancée, Dash had stopped using his key and rang the bell instead. Unless he knew he wouldn't be interrupting them. Linc's car in the driveaway had indicated he'd been safe to enter today. He had no desire to walk in on Xander and Sasha doing shit he didn't need to see.

"Dash! I didn't know you were here, too." Sasha flowed into the kitchen because that's what his brother's fiancee did. She glided across a room like the actress she was. Good thing she was equally down to earth, too.

"Hello, beautiful." He winked at her and caught Xander's glare.

Dash had every reason to suck up to Sasha. He'd crossed a line with Cassidy, Sasha's best friend and former personal assistant, despite both Xander and Sasha warning him against making a move. Things between them had escalated out of control after Sasha had been hurt by her stalker. Cassidy had needed a shoulder to cry on and Dash had been admittedly struck dumb from the first time he'd laid eyes on her.

He'd acted with his dick and all his other body parts that were drawn to the California girl. Their one night had blown his mind and even for a guy who'd had more than his share of women, that was a huge understatement.

He'd woken up as sober as when he'd slid into her the night before. No drunk excuses. Sunlight was streaming into the hotel room, illuminating her silky blonde hair, porcelain skin and delicate profile that would inspire songs in his future, and he'd freaked the fuck out. Instead of acting like a man, he'd dressed and disappeared before she woke up. Things had been awkward since.

"Knock knock, we're coming in!" Dash recognized Jagger, his lead guitarist's voice followed by footsteps, letting him know Mac, the bassist and Axel, the new drummer ... who happened to be Cassidy's brother, were with him. And fuck no, Axel did not know what had happened between Dash and his sister.

"In the kitchen," Dash called out.

"Really?" Xander asked, eyebrow raised in annoyance.

Sasha squeezed his shoulder. "It's fine."

"It's not. What's wrong with your house?" he asked Dash. "I love you but half the time it feels like you guys live here."

Dash lifted his shoulders. "Our road manager came by, called a few friends …"

"There's a party at his place," Mac said, as the guys filed into the kitchen dressed in bathing trunks and sneakers.

Sasha narrowed her gaze. "Where's Cass?"

Cassidy used to be Sasha's personal assistant until the band's latest one quit. Xander, Sasha and Harrison Dare, a movie star friend of hers, were creating a production company. But there was time before they'd need Cassidy to work. Axel had convinced her to lend he band a hand. Again, because Axel had no idea that Dash had fucked his sister and walked out, making certain she understood what one-and-done meant. Because yeah, when Dash got feelings, he was that much of an asshole.

"She's at the pool, keeping an eye on shit," Axel said, wincing under Sasha's pissed off glare.

Normally Dash would get the brunt of her anger but Axel had been the last guy to leave the house. And he was Cassidy's brother.

"You left her there with your goddamn entourage and the groupies?" Sasha walked over and smacked Dash upside the head.

"Hey! I didn't do it," he muttered.

She shot him a look that let him know he'd done other things to earn him that swat and he couldn't deny he deserved it. Nor could he fight with her in front of the band.

"Overseeing your parties and babysitting your groupies isn't part of her job description." Sasha swiped a set of car keys that sat on a bowl on the counter.

"Where are you going?" Xander asked.

"To save my best friend." She waved at Xander with a warm smile that Dash had to admit would make any man envious, ignored the rest of them, and strode out of the kitchen.

"Good job," Xander muttered. "Way to piss her off."

Dash ran a hand over his face. "Look I have a lot on my mind!"

Xander looked at him, his jaw tight and Dash didn't say a word. Of his two brothers, he could read Xander best. And Xander wanted to give Dash the same lecture Linc had.

When this nightmare was over, Dash needed to get his shit together. ASAP.

CASSIDY FORRESTER SAT on the edge of the saltwater, gunite pool, and dipped her feet into the warm water, ignoring the half naked groupies hanging onto men who were friends with Dash Kingston, the owner of the East Hampton home.

"I want a raise," she said out loud, to no one in particular. Because she sure as hell wasn't paid enough to babysit the entourage of the Original Kings, an award-winning rock band, comprised of man-child idiots who did what they wanted, when they wanted, everyone else be damned.

Her actual title was personal assistant to the band, a job she'd taken as a favor to her brother, their new drummer. The four core members had disappeared, leaving her to deal with the people, party, and mess they'd left behind. Nobody else would watch over the house and make sure these *guests* respected boundaries and stayed outside.

Not that Dash deserved anything from her, but her brother did.

"Hey, Cass," a familiar female voice said.

Cassidy glanced up, shading her eyes from the sun, just as her best friend Sasha Keaton, joined her, sitting by her side and also dipping her bare feet into the pool.

"What are you doing here? Shouldn't you be home with your hot fiancé?"

Sasha leaned back, her hands behind her on the bluestone patio. "When the guys showed up, I figured you'd want company."

Cassidy smiled. "And that's why I love you."

"Back at you," Sasha said, tilting her face towards the sun.

Sasha and Cassidy had been based in Los Angeles and traveled to locations where Sasha filmed until a couple of months ago, when Sasha had come to New York for a role. Cassidy, as her then personal assistant, had joined her. Sasha and Xander Kingston, Dash's brother and the author of the book on which the movie was based, had history they'd rekindled. After filming ended, Sasha had decided to move across the country to be with Xander and along with him, open a production company with another famous actor, Harrison Dare.

Cassidy planned to work for their new company, K-Talent, eventually but for now she'd agreed to help the band until they could hire someone they agreed on permanently.

"I came to take you to Xander's. You don't need to babysit the house," Sasha said.

"I take it the band made their way over there?" Cassidy asked.

Sasha nodded. "If they don't want to be here there's no reason for you to be, either. Let's go hang out at my place."

Cassidy grinned.

"What?"

"I like that you consider Xander's house, *your place*.

I'm glad you're happy." Her friend had soared to stardom, sacrificing her relationship with Xander in the process. But in the end, things had worked out for them and they both deserved it.

"I want the same thing for you. So while we're alone, I just wanted to make sure you're not upset with me," Sasha said. She lifted her feet out of the pool and they both stood and reached for towels on the chairs behind them.

"Why would I be?" Cassidy asked, while drying her legs.

Sasha did the same before sitting down to buckle her sandals as she replied. "I know you don't want to be around Dash but when Xander asked if the band could borrow your talents for a short time, I couldn't lie. It's going to take a while to get the paperwork for the new business going and Harrison is finishing up a movie. We all have down time now."

"I know. And I didn't have to say yes when Axel asked. This job isn't your doing. It's my brother's and that's because he has no idea I slept with Dash." Cassidy winced at the reminder of the best night of her life that had ended in the most humiliating morning after.

"I want to throttle Dash for being such an ass-hole," Sasha muttered.

There was nothing Cassidy could say to that since

she agreed. And if Axel found out, he'd kill Dash, himself.

Cassidy and Axel's parents had died in a car accident when Cassidy was five and Axel, seven. Their grandmother had raised them until she'd passed away, leaving an eighteen year old Axel to deal with Cassidy. A sixteen year old girl just finding herself. Though Cassidy felt like they'd looked out for each other, Axel had deemed himself her father figure and still acted as such.

Sasha sighed. "Yeah. I've seen how over protective Axel can be. I don't think he'd take the news well and the last thing you want is an issue between the band's lead singer and their new drummer. They have enough crazy publicity as it is," Sasha said.

"Agreed." Neither one of them mentioned Dash's baby scare out loud.

Sasha probably didn't want to hurt Cassidy by discussing it. And Cassidy didn't want to puke into the man's million dollar pool. She was aware based on the timing that he'd slept with the woman before he'd been with Cassidy. Not that it mattered. He hadn't been *with* her in any way that inspired loyalty or monogamy. But the thought of Dash fathering some skank's baby made Cassidy want to alternatively be sick and cry. How could she have let herself fall for the proverbial rock star?

A shriek came from the far side of the grass. Cassidy and Sasha turned to see one of the big breasted women pull off her bikini top and jump into the deep end of the pool. Three men shucked their shorts and followed.

"Oh. My. God." Cassidy spun away, not needing to see more.

"Come on. Let's get out of here." Sasha gathered her things and Cassidy pulled her cover-up over her bathing suit and slipped into her flip flops, happy to join her friend and leave this hedonistic nightmare behind.

DASH HUDDLED IN the corner of the overly large sofa in Xander's family room. While grumbling about too many people in his house, Xander had moved the band and Linc to a space with more sitting room. Status quo for his bestselling thriller author brother, whose books were made into hit movies, and liked a more solitary life.

Why Xander put up with Dash and his shit was beyond him. But Dash loved his older brother and always had. He'd pulled the same crap when they were kids, sleeping on the floor of Xander's bedroom until his mother bought a trundle bed so Dash was more comfortable.

Xander had grumbled then too, Dash thought wryly. But if his life went to hell, Xander would be there and not say *I told you so.*

Dash's cell rang, silencing everyone. He pulled out the phone from his pocket, glanced at the screen and his heart began to pound harder in his chest.

"It's the lawyer," he said to his audience, men he trusted with his life. Men who'd been waiting to hear the news along with him. The band for the publicity reasons Dash had thrust on them, and along with his brothers, they cared.

Palms slick with sweat, Dash took the call, putting it on speaker because he didn't want to have to repeat the news if was bad. "Peter, talk to me," he said to his attorney.

"Got the paternity results in my hand," the man said.

At that moment, Sasha walked in, Cassidy by her side. Because why shouldn't the woman who affected him on a soul deep level witness his humiliation?

Read **Just One Spark**.

Want even more Carly books?

CARLY'S BOOKLIST by Series – visit:
http://smarturl.it/CarlyBooklist

Sign up for Carly's Newsletter:
http://smarturl.it/carlynews

Join Carly's Corner on Facebook:
facebook.com/groups/SerendipitysFinest

Carly on Facebook:
facebook.com/CarlyPhillipsFanPage

Carly on Instagram:
instagram.com/carlyphillips

Carly's Booklist

The Dare Series

Dare to Love Series
Book 1: Dare to Love (Ian & Riley)
Book 2: Dare to Desire (Alex & Madison)
Book 3: Dare to Touch (Dylan & Olivia)
Book 4: Dare to Hold (Scott & Meg)
Book 5: Dare to Rock (Avery & Grey)
Book 6: Dare to Take (Tyler & Ella)
A Very Dare Christmas – Short Story (Ian & Riley)

** Sienna Dare gets together with Ethan Knight in **The Knight Brothers** (Dare Me Tonight).*

** Jason Dare gets together with Faith in the **Sexy Series** (More Than Sexy).*

Dare NY Series (NY Dare Cousins)
Book 1: Dare to Surrender (Gabe & Isabelle)
Book 2: Dare to Submit (Decklan & Amanda)
Book 3: Dare to Seduce (Max & Lucy)

The Knight Brothers
Book 1: Take Me Again (Sebastian & Ashley)
Book 2: Take Me Down (Parker & Emily)
Book 3: Dare Me Tonight (Ethan Knight & Sienna Dare)
Novella: Take The Bride (Sierra & Ryder)

Take Me Now – Short Story (Harper & Matt)

The Sexy Series
Book 1: More Than Sexy (Jason Dare & Faith)
Book 2: Twice As Sexy (Landon & Vivienne)
Book 3: Better Than Sexy (Tanner & Scarlett)
Novella: Sexy Love (Shane & Amber)

Dare Nation
Book 1: Dare to Resist (Austin & Quinn)
Book 2: Dare to Tempt (Damon & Evie)
Book 3: Dare to Play (Jaxon & Macy)
Book 4: Dare to Stay (Brandon & Willow)
Novella: Dare to Tease (Hudson & Brianne)

* Paul Dare's sperm donor kids

Kingston Family
Book 1: Just One Night (Linc Kingston & Jordan Greene)
Book 2: Just One Scandal (Chloe Kingston & Beck Daniels)
Book 3: Just One Chance (Xander Kingston & Sasha Keaton)
Book 4: Just One Spark (Dash Kingston & Cassidy Forrester)
Book 5: Just One Wish (Axel Forrester)
Book 6: Just One Dare (Aurora Kingston & Nick Dare)

Other Indie Series

Billionaire Bad Boys
Book 1: Going Down Easy
Book 2: Going Down Hard
Book 3: Going Down Fast
Book 4: Going In Deep
Going Down Again – Short Story

Hot Heroes Series
Book 1: Touch You Now
Book 2: Hold You Now
Book 3: Need You Now
Book 4: Want You Now

Bodyguard Bad Boys
Book 1: Rock Me
Book 2: Tempt Me
Novella: His To Protect

Carly's Originally Traditionally Published Books

The Chandler Brothers
Book 1: The Bachelor
Book 2: The Playboy
Book 3: The Heartbreaker

Hot Zone
Book 1: Hot Stuff

Book 2: Hot Number

Book 3: Hot Item

Book 4: Hot Property

Costas Sisters

Book 1: Under the Boardwalk

Book 2: Summer of Love

Lucky Series

Book 1: Lucky Charm

Book 2: Lucky Break

Book 3: Lucky Streak

Bachelor Blogs

Book 1: Kiss Me if You Can

Book 2: Love Me If You Dare

Ty and Hunter

Book 1: Cross My Heart

Book 2: Sealed with a Kiss

Carly Classics (Unexpected Love)

Book 1: The Right Choice

Book 2: Perfect Partners

Book 3: Unexpected Chances

Book 4: Suddenly Love

Book 5: Worthy of Love

Carly Classics (The Simply Series)

Book 1: Simply Sinful

Book 2: Simply Scandalous

Book 3: Simply Sensual

Book 4: Body Heat (not currently available)

Book 5: Simply Sexy

* Every book stands alone – missing Body Heat won't hurt series enjoyment

Carly's Still Traditionally Published Books

Serendipity Series

Book 1: Serendipity*

Book 2: Destiny

Book 3: Karma

* May be difficult to find.

Serendipity's Finest Series

Book 1: Perfect Fling

Book 2: Perfect Fit

Book 3: Perfect Together

Serendipity Novellas

Book 1: Fated*

Book 2: Perfect Stranger*

* May be difficult to find.

Stand-Alone Books

Brazen

Secret Fantasy

Seduce Me

The Seduction

More Than Words Volume 7 – Compassion Can't Wait

Naughty Under the Mistletoe

Grey's Anatomy 101 Essay

About the Author

NY Times, Wall Street Journal, and USA Today Bestseller, Carly Phillips is the queen of Alpha Heroes, at least according to The Harlequin Junkie Reviewer. Carly married her college sweetheart and lives in Purchase, NY along with her crazy dogs who are featured on her Facebook and Instagram pages. The author of over 75 romance novels, she has raised two incredible daughters and is now an empty nester. Carly's book, The Bachelor, was chosen by Kelly Ripa as her first romance club pick. Carly loves social media and interacting with her readers. Want to keep up with Carly? Sign up for her newsletter and receive TWO FREE books at www.carlyphillips.com.